W9-DFN-914

AUTUMN WORLD

AUTUMN WORLD

A NOVEL BY

JOAN MARIE VERBA
TESS MEARA
DEBORAH K. JONES
MARGARET HOWES
AND
RUTH BERMAN

FTL PUBLICATIONS
MINNETONKA MINNESOTA

FTL Publications
P O Box 1363
Minnetonka, MN 55345-0363
www.ftlpublications.com
FTL_Publications@compuserve.com

Cover design and artwork by Terry Miller and Rita Miller at ImagiMation 3D, www.im3d.com.
Cover copyright © 2000 by Joan Marie Verba

Printed in the United States of America.

Reprinted May 2002.

ISBN 0-9653575-3-8

Previously published by Stone Dragon Press, 2000. First printing, 2001.

DEDICATION

to the other members of the Aaardvark Writing Group

with special thanks to Eleanor Arnason and Eric M. Heideman
for help in universe-building,
and to
Ellen and Mary Kuhfeld for criticism.

CRASHLANDING

Woke and felt delicate clawed hands touching her. Mandibles clicked. She recognized the sound.

Voices—high and thin with an odd breathless quality—cried, "Leah! Wake up! Come to! For us! For me!"

Opened her eyes. Saw sunlight, shining through orange and yellow foliage. She tried to move. It hurt. She groaned.

"Are you injured? Is it fatal?"

She tried to think of an answer. Words did not come. A head rose into view. Triangular with compound eyes. Feathery antennae. Mandibles inset with jewels. The mandibles moved. Click! Click! The jewels flashed.

"What?" she asked.

"A crash," the voices said. "All dead! The Jheehan. The Hultzu. One of me. Maybe two. I hurt. I am in pain. I feel less intelligent."

Shit!

The voices went on. "The Jheehan looks like a piece of pita bread. The Hultzu has bones sticking out all over. I won't describe what I look like."

She got up on one elbow. She was in a clearing. The ground was covered with something that looked like moss. It was burgundy red.

The person—her comrade—the one other survivor—stood around her in a circle. Four dark bodies, each one a meter long. The antennae waved anxiously. The heads were lifted high, as were the short, round torsos. The front pair of legs, which ended in a pair of claws or pincers, moved nervously, picking at moss or reaching out to her, touching lightly. The pincers clicked like the mandibles but far more quietly.

Each body had three segments: head, torso, and rear, which was shaped like a torpedo or a beetle. The rear segment rested on three pairs of legs. Four of the legs were thick and solid. The last pair was long and narrow and tended to drag. The mating legs.

A comforting sight. Familiar. Though it bothered her to see only four bodies. There ought to be five.

Who was gone? She looked at the heads. Mandibles clicked. Gems glittered. Diamond was here. Topaz. Garnet. Peridot. The missing body was Tourmaline.

"Who is in pain?" she asked.

"I am," said a voice.

Other voices said, "Garnet."

"I am dying," Garnet said.

She looked at the body that had spoken last. At first, it seemed like the others. Then she noticed that one of the legs was bent at an odd angle. The antennae barely moved. The mandibles were entirely motionless. And there was something about the stance of the creature that indicated pain, though she couldn't figure out what it was.

"Is there anything I can do?"

"No," said Garnet.

The others repeated, "No."

She pushed herself up into a sitting position. Oh, Peace! Everything ached. Maybe she was dying, too. Her eyes kept going in and out of focus. And she felt heavy. Was that the weight of mortality? Then she remembered the planet was larger than Earth and had a stronger gravitational field.

"Are you all right?" her companion asked. "Do you plan to die?"

"I don't think so." She tried to get her eyes in focus. There were trees at the edge of the clearing. They had gray trunks that were scaled like fish. Their foliage was lacy. The sky was brilliant blue. She could not see any clouds. "What happened?"

"I don't know. We don't know. The Jheehan was piloting. All at once, ka-boom! I hurt. I cannot think clearly. I am less intelligent than I used to be."

She got up on her knees. Her head felt peculiar. "Where are we?"

"We—I—don't know. Down. On the planet. Are you going to be able to stand?"

"There's one way to find out."

The bodies moved in around her. She felt hard shells. Pincers. Antennae. They were trying to hold her.

"Okay," she said and got up on her feet. She swayed. The bodies moved back.

"Radio," she said.

"Broken," said a voice.

Another voice said, "We tried."

"Too far for speaking," a third voice said.

Speaking meant telepathy. A skill—an ability—which Earthers did not have. The Jheehan could have spoken to another Jheehan or one of the dolphins at the base, but the Jheehan was dead.

"The ship?" she asked.

"This way." They scurried ahead of her—all except Garnet, who remained motionless.

She looked at it—or him—or her. "Is there anything?"

"No," said Garnet. "Go on."

Beyond the trees was a slope leading to a river. Burnt vegetation. Smoke rising. Congealing foam. Twisted metal. The body of the Hultzu. It must have crawled out of the ship to die.

She went down on her knees and vomited. Her companion made a noise like a meadow full of crickets. Chirps of unhappiness.

She finished vomiting. She got up and stumbled to the river. She rinsed her mouth and washed her face. When she was done, she said, "We have to bury them."

"Let me. Let us. You are injured. You are in distress."

"I'm all right. I think. You lost Tourmaline."

Her companion said nothing. She splashed water on her neck. "We need something to dig with."

"We—I—will get," her companion said.

She sat by the river and waited. It was wide and smooth. On the far side was a forest, yellow and orange. Animals flew over the water. They fluttered like bats. Catching bugs, most likely.

Her companion came back with a shovel and a pick. Odd. The kinds of things that Admin decided to put on a shuttle plane. The tools must belong to some kind of emergency kit.

"Here," she said. It was a good place for a grave. The gentle slope was covered with a lacy yellow plant a meter high. Small flying bugs darted above the vegetation. A good place to lie for however long. Would the microbes here be able to feed on alien flesh and bone? Who knew?

She dug. Her companion helped, digging with pincers, chirping. The grave was shallow. She didn't have the energy for a deep one. After she finished, she went to get the Hultzu. It was covered with blood. The blood was copper-based and green. White pieces of bone came through the skin. This mess had been a lovely, elegant, intelligent being. What Earther could move with the grace of a Hultzu? What Earther had a voice that always sang?

She dragged the Hultzu to the grave and pushed it in. Then she went looking for the Jheehan.

Her companion was right. The Jheehan did look like a piece of pita bread. Or else like a fur rug. She looked at the body, spread on the floor of the control room, then turned and walked out.

"Can you take it to the grave?" she said to her companion.

"Yes. I—we—can."

"Good. I can't. I'm going to sit by the river. I think I've had a concussion."

Peridot came with her and crouched next to her, touching her anxiously, chirping.

"How did it happen?" she asked. "I'm fine. I think I'm fine. Bruised a little." She moved and winced. "Well, maybe—bruised a lot. But I'm alive. I don't have a cut. I don't have a broken bone. And they are dead. Why?"

"Not good on philosophy," said Peridot. "Can't think clearly."

They watched the river. The bat-like creatures fluttered back and forth. A dark shape surfaced way out in the water. Only for a moment. She couldn't make out what it was. But it was large.

"Done," said a voice.

She looked around. Topaz was back. "Come. Cover with dirt."

She went back to the grave. There were two bodies in it. "Where is Tourmaline?"

"Take care," said a voice. "We—I—take care."

They were a notoriously private species. No one knew what lay under their gleaming shells. No one knew for certain if the shells were natural or artificial. She remembered hearing once—they were like roaches. You never saw a dead one unless you sprayed.

The remark was racist. Why had she remembered it? Thank Justice! They could not read her mind.

She buried the Hultzu and the Jheehan. When she was done, she stuck the shovel upright in the soft dirt. She wiped her hands on her coverall. "I've never buried anyone before."

"No?" asked her companion.

"I grew up in a space station. People got recycled for organ and tissue donation. Every part of our bodies can be transplanted or transformed into stem cells. We didn't go to the Recycling Area. Instead, we went to one of the Recreational Areas and held a wake."

"What?" asked her companion.

"A party. To celebrate what the person had done for the station—and what they were going to do. Nothing is ever wasted in a station."

Her companion said nothing.

"What about Garnet?" she asked.

"Dead," said her companion. "We take care. Of Garnet. Of Tourmaline. Wait here."

They scurried off. She sat down. Time passed. Shadows lengthened. The sky developed a late afternoon color.

Peridot came back. "Done. Almost done."

She wondered how they went about disposing of dead members of their species. She wasn't going to ask. Her field was sociology and linguistics, but she didn't feel like a scholar at the moment. She felt tired and confused.

Peridot touched her with a pincer. It was a gesture of comfort—or maybe a gesture that asked for comfort. She laid a hand on the hard slick torso. It felt warm. Peridot chirped.

She dozed a little, leaning against her companion, dreaming of walking in a wood of trees with fish-scale bark. Sweat trickled down her back. Her shoe rubbed against her foot. Damn! Damn! She'd be limping soon.

The wood ended before a slope that led down to a river. The river was called the Angin. The slope was covered by a plant called golden lace.

"Wake!" cried Peridot.

"What?"

She stumbled up and turned, lurching away from Peridot.

Earthers. No. It could not be. Not here. Not in armor that glittered in the sun. They came down the yellow slope. Light flashed off the blades of their drawn weapons, the coils of their whips. They were upright. Bipedal. Their arms were bare of clothing or fur. Their skin was blue. They did not have the grace of a Hultzu. They stumbled and jumped like her own people. She looked into the eyes of the one who led.

A door opened in her mind. But of course! Now I see! I understand! I didn't know!

She held out her hands, open. The palms were forward Look. No weapons. "We come in peace," she said. Peridot had not moved.

Disgust. Fear. Longing. The staring purple eyes of the alien seemed to absorb her whole consciousness. Blackness closed in. She felt her body hit the earth. She could not move, but she could still hear.

"Tie her up," said a voice. "Rig a stretcher. We are taking her to the City." The language was not Earthan. She could not possibly understand it. But she did.

More of them were coming. The first man shone beyond her closed lids as irresistible as the sun. His presence was the last thread tying her to consciousness. She struggled to rise through darkness.

Her vision cleared. She was standing, but the height was wrong. One of the men was kicking Peridot. No!

Sight deserted her again. She was still lying on the ground. They were hurting Peridot. Must move!

A whip thong lashed Peridot's head.

She screamed, "No!"

Peridot! Have to get up? Peridot!

"No!"

THE TWINS

It was nine days since they had left Oshune. The hive buzz of the city's thoughts had faded on the third day. On the fourth and fifth, the minds of spouses and kin had passed beyond contact. On the sixth day all but the Blessed had lost touch with their twins who remained behind, and since morning day before yesterday even the identical twins of the Blessed were out of reach.

Matvar looked with cold eyes on his shivering troop as they jogged off their sleepiness in the chill dawn mist. Half of them were paired and content, but few of the rest had ever been beyond twintouch in their lives. Their emanations were shadowed with the pain of this new, terrifying loneliness.

Matvar was not moved. One day the troop would return within range, and all these men would be twinned again. For Matvar, there would never be such a homecoming. The dead are forever out of reach.

He pushed the men for their own good. Better their attention should be on the demands of the body, here and now, than on lost kindred. Even the officers were made to lead their mounts and go on foot until the day warmed or they reached their objective.

In spite of the mist, the morning promised to be fine. Spring had taken hold even here in the high country, where shreds of snow endured only in the deepest shade. Fresh yellow firn was springing up everywhere through the dark litter of winter's leaves. On the newly bared limbs of the trees, the leaves of summer were beginning to unfold, orange and moon-gold.

By the fourth kroon, the mist had burnt off, and the sun looked down out of a cloudless blue. The men stopped beyond a small stream where the trail began to ascend more steeply toward a ridge topped with a spine of crumbling rock.

Matvar sent for the guide. "Is this the ridge?" he asked.

"Yes, your Honor." The man kept his forehead carefully close to the dust on which he knelt. "The thing can be seen from the top."

"And how long to get down to it?"

"Not long, your Blessedness. It is half a kroon, no more."

Matvar's lip curled at the title. He fingered the handle of his whip, then let his hand drop. There was no way the man could know. "Lead on," he ordered.

The path appeared to be nothing more than a dry watercourse lined solidly with brambles. The men toiled heavily upward, booted feet sliding on shards of stone that littered the trail. The first time his kurval stumbled, Matvar dismounted and went on foot like the rest. The guide, a local man, scrambled ahead nimbly, passing out of sight in a few moments. They heard him calling from above.

At the top of the ridge, there was a gap in the stone rampart, a narrow pass wide enough for Matvar and his lieutenants to stand together. The guide knelt on the ground, waiting. Labek, Matvar's second, raised his arm and pointed at the object they could all see in the forest below.

A long scar of ruin cut the trees from southwest to northeast, toward a loop of the river. Where it ended, at the edge of a golden lace meadow, there was a twisted mass, veiled in smoke.

"That is the thing we saw," said Labek. "The sky fire."

The guide vigorously gestured confirmation. Matvar grunted, his blue face expressionless. Behind him the men crowded forward to see and whisper among themselves.

Finally, Arunesh spoke, somewhat diffidently. "My lord, I have heard of rocks falling from the sky, making such a fire as we saw last night."

Matvar did not take his eyes from the thing. "Does that look like a rock to you?"

"No, my lord," Arunesh answered regretfully.

"We will go down," said Matvar.

The descent of the ridge was no easier than the ascent had been. The trail was even steeper. Matvar knew they were exposed to the sight of anyone below, but there was no other way down through the dense thorn. The men had their hands close to their weapons before he mentally ordered them to. They did not speak aloud. Their uneasiness filled the air like the vanished mist.

After the troop reassembled in the cover of the forest's edge, Matvar sent two of the men ahead to find an approach and take a closer look. The officers took to their kurvals again and put up the war crests on their helmets.

The scouts returned shortly.

"It is not a rock, my lord. It looks like a huge creature made of metal."

"Like an insect, my lord, with legs. It is all ruined, half burned."

"There has been burning all around. Some little fires are still alight. We did not go into the burned area."

"We saw much white stuff over the burn, like sea foam. We did not touch it. Perhaps it is that great creature's blood."

Matvar knew the others could feel his agitation, as he could feel theirs. Their minds shared the scouts' confused images: the giant insect body smashed into the earth; the white, jelly-like blood congealing upon the charred forest. And these were not the whole.

Matvar was greatly disturbed. He asked, "Did you see no smaller creatures? Could this insect thing be a vessel?"

"No, my lord."

But the answer was a denial of the remembered images, of buckled metal, of seared ceramic. The opening in the body that was no wound, but a door.

A door! The guide crouched on the ground, sobbing quietly. Matvar and his men met the shock unbroken but with no less fear. None of them had ever expected to come face to face with the Teachings. The Starborn, the Sky Dwellers. They who abandoned us in the dawn of time.

Matvar silently collected their attention and waited until every face turned toward him. "Hear me," he said. "This is Crowns business. Everything we find is to be treated as if it is holy. We will take this news to Oshune. Their Holinesses will make a determination."

In spite of the fear he could not entirely conceal from his men, Matvar felt a tiny exhilaration. This was his. He—formerly Blessed, now untwinned, disgraced, reduced to this low duty of provincial peace-keeping and tax collection—what if he was to be the one to bring word before the Twin Thrones that the Sky Dwellers had returned?

What if he was to be the one to redeem the ancient Faith? To expose the Veen faction for the heresy it was? Words of prophecy began to rise from his memory. Was it not foretold the messenger would be one abandoned by the Blessing of the Gods?

He was careful to guard these thoughts from the others. In spite of all his vigilance, it was still possible there were Veen spies in the troop. Such a spy would not even remember his mission until the right circumstances triggered the deeply-planted commands that made an unsuspected man into a traitor.

He had no confidence that a Veen heretic would be awed or converted with evidence of the ancient true Faith before his eyes. It did not matter if Ashven herself walked out of the thing in the forest. The Veen were not beyond destroying any evidence that threatened their expanding power in the name of the Twin Thrones. Nor were they beyond slaughtering every witness to such evidence.

Matvar wondered how many of his men could be trusted. The best course open to him was to return to the capital quickly, before the images faded, and with physical proof if possible. There were too many witnesses for a man alone, or even a handful of men, to prevent the news from reaching Oshune. Only if all of them were traitors would the vindication of the Faith be concealed.

Without audible command, he led them to the edge of the fire clearing. Hands moved in prayer signs as the men beheld the object with their own eyes. It was a vessel, unlike the pictures of the Teachings, to be sure, but clearly a made artifact of Sky Dwellers, a Star Ship.

There was no sign of the Sky Dwellers themselves. It did not seem possible that any being could have survived that wreck and fire. Yet the door was open. Broken and burned as the ship was, it was not destroyed.

Matvar was uneasy. A Sky Dweller, safely dead, convenient on the ground at some distance from the ship—that would be best. A corpse would be easy to carry back to Oshune. It was less comfortable to think of Sky Dwellers alive, watching, perhaps taking offense. Matvar was not eager to go inside to look for them.

With a few gestures and silent commands, he divided the troop into three parts. He put Labek and Arunesh in charge of two of the groups (Why not? They were both brought up in the Old Faith) and took the third himself. Arunesh would remain with his men at this spot while the other two-thirds would circle the wreck in opposite directions, looking for signs of life—or death—and anything of interest.

With a salute, Labek led his men to the left as Matvar took his to the right. It was difficult going. Many trees were down, as if felled by a cyclone wind from the vessel. Some still smoldered. The white stuff lay over everything that had burned, and none of the men had any desire to touch it. They almost lost sight of the wreck several times, seeing it only as a high, bulky shadow through foam-covered trees and scrub.

Twice Matvar sent pairs of men to force their way inward, to try to glimpse the thing from the new angle and bring back images. This was only partly successful. The foam was more dense there, festooned in hideous loops between branches and piled in mounds below. It veiled the ship and prevented close approach.

They had labored nearly halfway around. The sound of the river was audible above the wind-rustle of the trees. An increase in daylight ahead indicated the nearness of the meadow. The view would be better there. The men moved cautiously toward the open space. They stopped suddenly and glanced uneasily at each other.

There was someone in the clearing, not one of the men; it was a female. Only her grief came to them at that distance and, under it, a uniform anxiety not quite fear. She was not sending, and she was not aware of their presence. Her emanations were weak, those of a singlet who had led an isolated life. A lack of social reinforcement would explain why the soldiers had not detected her sooner.

There were such people who lived in the hinterlands—odd, simple folk, shunning the society of others. No doubt this woman was such a one. Perhaps the Star Ship had come down on her rude home or her only companion. She was grieving for someone or something.

Matvar signaled his men to spread out around the perimeter of the clearing as they approached. The female must not be allowed to get away before he had a chance to question her. It would not be wise to allow her to carry a lot of nonsense to the other locals.

He came to the last screen of branches and stopped in astonishment. To his left, the ruined vessel loomed up, crumpled and blackened. It invaded the clearing here, so there had been less fire. Before it, the ground had been disturbed. There was a long, shallow mound of piled dirt. Half obscured by the golden lace, a figure knelt next to something with gems that flashed in the sun.

She was not human. Her body was long, narrow, sharp-jointed. Her flesh was odd, the color of fungus or insect larvae, and her hair, if it was hair, was colored like bhesh-wood, hanging down in waving strands. A Sky Dweller she must be, but there was nothing like her in the Teachings. She was ugly, a grotesque mimicry of human form.

As Matvar stepped forward into the meadow, she slowly got to her feet, turned, and raised her misshapen head. Her eyes met his. Only then did she know she was not alone.

Surprise. Vast surprise. I did not know. I did not know. Who are you? Who? I did not know!

She stood frozen, staring. Her thoughts were nauseatingly incoherent. Only her surprise was clear. And her discovery of ignorance. "I did not know I was human." "I did not know you existed." "I did not know I could speak." "I did not know the nature of communication." All of these meanings were present, and more that Matvar could not fathom.

He was sick with shock. Her thought-touch was Rudvar's. Since the hell-blasted day his brother slipped beyond the Veil of Ashven, no one had touched Matvar so, no one had entered the twintouch with him. Now, this creature from the sky spoke to him in the mind-voice of his dead twin. It was an obscenity, a blasphemy.

His first impulse was to kill her. If he had been alone he might have, Starborn or not. But he was not alone, and as he made his men move forward into the clearing, he was aware of a longing, years dead, awakening to howl within him. He had forgotten what it felt like, the intimacy of twinship.

She had never known, it seemed, for she took no notice of the need that shook him. His impulse to do her harm met only bewilderment. She displayed unnaturally formed hands, weaponless. Words came out of her mouth. Matvar understood them. "We are harmless." We?

Pain welled up inside Matvar, into a place long empty. The pain was better than the emptiness. Harmless? She needed no weapon to tear at him. The pain was too sharp to bear, but it was too late to kill her.

She was like an infant. She had no defenses. Matvar hunted for her sleep lock, although it made him gag to do so. He found it and touched it lightly. Her eyes closed, and she collapsed to the ground, breathing softly and peacefully. Her conscious level was smooth and clear; she was asleep. Matvar drew a deep breath to compose himself before the men.

"Bind her," he commanded. "Make a litter. We will carry her to Oshune."

Labek's group approached, agog with curiosity. Labek was disconcerted to have missed the excitement.

"A Sky Dweller?" he asked.

"I do not know," Matvar replied.

"What is that thing?"

Matvar turned. He had forgotten the large glittering object over which the woman had been kneeling. Now all of the men were gathered around it except the few in charge of the female. He pushed his way through the ring, followed by Labek.

The thing was about half as long as a man's height, made in the shape of a giant insect. It was fashioned from an iridescent gold-green substance set with hundreds of colored gems arranged in a complex pattern. The eyes were faceted spheres the size of a fist. It was a magnificent artifact. If the hierarchs of the Old Faith rejoiced at the Sky Dweller, the Crowns would be equally intrigued by this treasure.

Labek knelt down and touched the jeweled carapace. He pulled his hand back quickly with a shout. "I am burned!" He jumped to his feet and kicked the shining thing savagely.

One of the sparkling antennae quivered visibly. A gilt leg moved slowly, then another. The men stepped back. "It moved! " "It is alive!" they gasped to one another.

The creature scrabbled feebly with several of its legs and turned toward Labek, who backed away nursing his hand. One of its antennae whipped across his face. He screamed and pulled his whip from his belt. Before Matvar could stop him, he lashed the creature across the head, laying open one of the glittering eyes.

A shriek tore the air. Matvar turned. The woman-thing was awake, struggling to rise against the thongs that bound her. She screamed again, the same alien syllable. Her meaning of horror and denial emanated with an unexpected power. Matvar put her under again quickly, with reinforcement from several of the more skilled men. It was sickening. He hoped it would not be necessary again soon.

The insect raised its front end off the ground, waving legs and antennae. It balanced briefly, shivering, then toppled to the side and rolled onto its back. The eight legs twitched a few times, then pulled in close to the body. The creature did not stir again.

Labek fell to his knees, moaning. A dripping wound crossed one side of his face, missing the eye by a finger-breadth. The hand with which he had touched the insect was blistered.

"See to him," Matvar ordered two of the men. "Wash his hurts with water. He may be poisoned."

He found a long stick and poked at the jeweled body. It did not move. "I think it is dead," he said. "It had no emanations. It was not sentient. It was an animal, perhaps the pet of this other."

He glanced at the female, who still slept curled on her side. The men stooped to lift her onto an improvised litter of branches. Against his disgust of her, he searched for any sign she was returning to consciousness, found none, and nodded to her bearers to continue. He noticed they touched her warily and wore their battle gloves.

He raised his voice so all the men could hear him and sent a stern warning to their minds. "We will take this other creature's body back with us also. No man is to touch it. The punishment is pain. You have seen. These beings are Crowns' business and are to be treated as if they are sacred.

"Here. You and you, and you two. Make a bier with branches. Roll the animal on without touching it, even with gloves."

He sent to Arunesh, who was restless with curiosity. All the men in the watch party had received images of shock and violence and knew that there had been a wounding. Their minds clamored for news. Matvar sent a few images and the command to wait, to continue watching the door of the Star Ship.

He called one of the men who had been in Labek's party and took a report from him. There was very little to hear. The other group had seen no sign of life or any artifacts outside the ship's burn.

When they returned at last to Arunesh and the rest of the troop, the sun was high overhead. Arunesh had nothing to report. With Labek disabled, he was second-in-command and tried to hide his self-importance.

"Will we enter the ship, my lord?"

"No. Our duty is to take back this news. We have sufficient proof." He nodded at the two litters, which the men had laid down among the trees. "The authorities will decide what else is to be done."

"Yes, my lord." Arunesh sketched a prayer sign. "Are there further instructions, my lord?"

"We return to the inn where we spent last night. The men are not to speak or send to anyone about this, not even their twins."

"Yes, my lord." Arunesh moved away to pass these orders on to the rest of the troop.

A short time later, they were ready to move. Labek, who was feverish and barely conscious, was tied to his kurval. There was no change in the two beings from the ship. Matvar led the way out of the forest and up the rocky path to the top of the ridge.

He had climbed no more than halfway when there was a shout from below. His eyes searched for the image sent from the rear guard. He found it: another giant insect creature like the dead one, scuttling toward them through the edge of the wood at the foot of the hill.

The men raised a cry and drew their blades. The creature stopped. Its antennae trembled. Then it spun around with unexpected grace and sped away along the bottom of the slope. The sun flashed upon its jeweled back and glittered from a different source farther back among the trees.

"Another one!" Arunesh exclaimed. "My lord, there are two more of them alive."

"Let them go," Matvar said. All twinned things were under the Blessing of the Gods. Let the Crowns deal with this.

The men lowered their weapons. As they watched, the two sparkling creatures passed side by side into the shade of the trees and disappeared.

ESCAPE FROM THE INN

With Valad a two days' ride behind her, Thiele felt secure enough to stay the night at an inn. After seeing that her riding ornit, Beast, was properly stabled, she went inside. It was a comfortable two-story building made of hightower planks, whose common room had a large fireplace and a high ceiling supported by plamon beams. Thiele paid her fee to the porter, put her travel bag in her bedroom, washed, and went back to the main room. There she settled in a large padded chair to rest until the evening meal was ready.

There were only three other people in the room, all men. One was sitting in a chair on the other side of the room, reading a devotional tract on astrology, while two others spoke in low voices by the fireplace. Thiele could hear voices and clanking sounds through an open door in the back and smelled food cooking. The low hum of mental images from the others, unreadable unless she made an effort to do so, played in her mind. She leaned back and relaxed but fingered the strap of her carry pack to reassure herself it was still there. Her first floor room was locked, and if anyone tried to steal her clothes, it was no great loss; however, she had worked very hard and come a long way to scavenge the electronic components from the Mullen Ruins, and no one was going to take them from her. Even though they were of no value to anyone in this region, thieves usually snatched anything not tied down and evaluated the contents later.

So she put her mind at rest, sensing that no one was trying to contact her. It was a short respite: the door soon opened and a group of soldiers came in. Thiele straightened up, guarding her thoughts, afraid at first that Valad had sent some of his men ahead, but a short examination told her they were not Valad's people. A longer look made her start. She suppressed her reaction so no one would get suspicious and read her mind during her excitement.

There, between two soldiers, was a being the like of which she had seen only in illustrations. Thiele determined the being was female, though two of her four breasts were oversized. Or, perhaps, she only had two. Her skin lacked blue or purple tones; it was strictly a shade of brown. She stood above the soldiers and was quite thin. Even so, she moved slowly, causing Thiele to look for chains or leg restraints. There weren't any. She wondered if the being were sick or dazed.

As the soldiers stood there, one supported by a companion as if wounded, their commander arranged for rooms with the porter. Thiele touched the being's mind. The thoughts were confused, like a child's. But there was one strong image of two green insects scrambling away. Now, why would the being think of insects? Thiele withdrew, thinking it was best not to draw attention to herself. The being seemed too confused to be aware of Thiele reading her mind, fortunately.

The soldiers left the room. Thiele followed with her thoughts until they secured the being in a ground floor room three doors from her own and set a guard outside. The remaining soldiers went to their rooms. None were aware of Thiele's telepathic surveillance.

While Thiele thought over what to do, the guard commander returned. As the porter handed him his receipts, Thiele strolled to the desk. Peering at the ledger, she saw his signature and learned his name. Agund Matvar. It was an old Oshune name. The Agund were a large clan, mostly military, not in the Veen camp, as far as she knew. He turned, folding the papers carefully before putting them in a pocket.

She struck up a conversation. "Evening's greeting, Commander. I saw your men bring in someone tonight. A prisoner, perhaps?"

She sensed he didn't want to answer, but he wanted even less to appear rude in front of strangers. "No. We found her on the road, dazed. Half-witted, maybe."

As casually as possible, Thiele said, "Such deformities are common among the people of the deep woods at the bend of the Angin northwest of here. That is not far off my route. Would you like me to take her home?"

The man barely suppressed his alarm at her suggestion.

Thiele pretended not to have noticed.

"Duty requires me to bring her in to the magistrate, as orders dictate for any stranger without papers," he said calmly. "No doubt one of her own people will claim her later." The last sentence was almost a mumble.

"No doubt."

"I thank you for identifying her home for me, Learned One. You have been of help." He walked away.

It seemed to Thiele that he had been anxious to end the conversation. If so, it might have looked suspicious to him if she had tried to continue it. She regretted that, for if she had been able to speak with him long enough, telepathic nuances would have let her guess whether his intention to turn the being over to the local magistrate was a serious one. If so, an even longer conversation might have allowed her to subtly persuade him to hand the being over to her. As it was, the only thing she knew for certain was he did not want Thiele to take the being with her. This reaction opened up a whole spectrum of possibilities, but she did not intend to stay around him long enough to find out what those possibilities might be. Whatever the reason for his alarm at her suggestion, one thing was certain: she could not risk even the possibility that he might hand the being over to the local magistrate. The local magistrate was Valad, the one she was trying to get away from. It would be doubly bad for the being if Valad found her. Doubly bad.

Thiele left the common room immediately after eating. No one seemed to notice. Telepathically scanning from her own room, she found that after dinner, the guard had changed and the others in the troop had retired. In the common room she found only a few people remaining, conversing in low tones. Taking her bag and packs, Thiele opened the door of her room and stepped out into the hall.

The guard was staring straight ahead, not at her. He would expect to pick up a telepathic impression if someone was approaching, but Thiele could do what few others could: suppress her thought impressions completely. Treading softly, she stepped within arm's length of the guard. Reaching to the back of his neck, she touched a pressure point and overwhelmed his mind so he would not cry out, even telepathically. Once that was done, she implanted a hypnotic suggestion. She put her hand down. The guard would stand there, staring, until morning, with no memory of her other than perhaps the touch of her hand.

Thiele took the keys from the guard and opened the door. She stepped inside.

The being backed slowly towards the far wall as Thiele softly closed the door. The prisoner stood still and silent as Thiele put down the packs and straightened up. Now Thiele performed what she privately called her "peace and friendship" routine. She put her arms at her side, palms out and facing toward the being. As a further sign of trust, she closed her eyes and leaned back. Then she sent out a flood of soothing, accepting thought impressions, hoping the being would recognize them as such. She pictured holding the being in her arms, stroking the being gently, making comforting sounds. After keeping this up for a short time, she sensed the being creeping towards her. Thiele was not afraid—she had a lock on the being's mind and could react swiftly at the first hostile intention. The being merely brushed Thiele's cheek with a fingertip--a peaceful gesture that Thiele had hoped for.

Thiele's eyes fluttered open. She relaxed her hold on the being a little. The being eyed her with an attitude of curiosity. Eyes open, Thiele now sent another thought-picture of her and the being astride Beast, riding away from the inn. The being flinched, at first, at the illusion of Beast in her mind, but her thoughts settled quickly. Now Thiele sent out the climax of her planned tableau: the vision of a busy spaceport with craft rising to the moons and beyond. It was conjured up from Thiele's imagination based on her readings plus a mural in a building back where she lived. She added an abstraction: a sinusoidal wave extending from the ground to the largest moon. She varied the wavelength and frequency of the abstraction to underscore her knowledge of the physics of light. To conclude, she conjured up the picture of an individual at one end of the wave talking into a sound-sender while an individual at the other end of the wave listened. Thiele sensed she had the being's undivided attention.

The moment of truth was at hand. Thiele reached into a pack. She slowly brought out a tiny circuit board, unwrapped it, and held it out in the being's direction. The being inched forward, touching Thiele's hand lightly as if to steady it. She scrutinized the electronics closely, then looked into Thiele's eyes. Thiele closed her hand and returned the part to her pack. She shouldered her packs and extended a hand to the being. The being took it. Thiele led her into the hallway.

The being stared at the guard while Thiele relocked the door and put the key back on his belt. To show he was harmless, Thiele waved a hand close to his face. He didn't flinch, though he blinked normally. Thiele took the being by the hand to lead her to the side door. A few steps showed Thiele that the being wasn't moving fast enough: what if someone came into the hall? She adjusted the packs so they covered her chest. After sending a picture to the being to show what she had planned, she took the being's arms and wrapped them around her neck. The being cooperated. Thiele hooked her arms behind the being's knees and lifted her. As Thiele suspected, the being was light. When she got to the door, she jogged the handle with an elbow and walked out, pushing the door shut behind her with a foot.

No one was outside; no one was near the stables. Thiele carried the being to the barn door and set her down. After taking off the packs, she went inside to saddle Beast. When she led him out, the being stared. Thiele picked up mental images of two strange animals and two mental pseudo-sounds, "camel," "ostrich."

Thiele turned to Beast. He looked a little like each, but also unlike both. She faced the being again. The being put a hand, outspread, on her chest. "Leah," she said, with an identifying thought impression.

Thiele caught the telepathic nuance. She imitated the gesture. "Thiele." She sent a picture to her showing how to mount Beast. Leah followed the mental instructions, but in the end, Thiele had to push her up into the saddle. Then Thiele hooked on her bag and packs. She mounted behind Leah, taking the reins.

"Go, Beast," she said. Beast started off. Leah grunted at the sudden up-and-down motion but soon settled into the rhythm.

Thiele checked behind them telepathically. No one followed; no alarm went out.

Thiele considered the route ahead. The road they were now on ran for a long stretch to a crossroads. They would not leave prints on the road, so they'd be almost impossible to track. Thiele reckoned that by sunrise, they could reach an abandoned woodcutter's shack, which was off the road and into the forest. By that time, the troop behind her would be hard pressed to get even a mental impression from her.

Leah sent an acknowledgment. Thiele responded soothingly. Either Leah was learning fast, or her telepathic instincts were good. Thiele was pleased.

Beast had now reached his traveling stride, which was smoother than his accelerating stride. With three moons out, there was enough light for Beast's eyes. Thiele scanned ahead and sensed the road was empty of travelers for a long stretch. There was thick forest on either side of the road; even there Thiele sensed nothing moving but wildlife. They were safe from animal attack; Thiele could manage them quite easily. Even highway robbers seldom challenged her, knowing her people carried little of value to them.

The night was cool, but not uncomfortably so. Leah settled herself back on Thiele's shoulder; her body was light and warm against her. Thiele sensed Leah was also accustomed to these temperatures. Chipits chirped softly in the forest undergrowth. Sakerets cooed as they hunted for their dinner. One flew silhouetted against the face of the largest moon. Twigs snapped and rustled; a larger animal or two was running in the woods. The air was soft, moist, and sweet-smelling. An intermittent breeze rustled the firn and plumiole.

Leah seemed to have been lulled into sleep. Thiele turned her thoughts inward to her dealings with Valad. She had first met him after her initial visit to the Mullen Ruins. In her travels, she would sleep where she could: in the open, at an inn, or at the outbuildings of a great estate; so when she had come to the gate of Valad's southern mansion, she had expected to be directed to a shed in the servant's quarters. Instead, the butler led her inside the mansion, where she was bathed and fed in great elegance. Afterwards, she was escorted to Valad's own rooms. There, by the fire, he slowly took off Thiele's shoes and stockings to bathe and caress her feet. She had been braced for a sexual advance, but he asked no more of her. Thiele was relieved, since she had hoped to woo a man of her own people, Palmo, when she was ready to conceive.

Valad had let her go the next day, but each time she came into his sector, he had sent out his men to fetch her back to his northern or southern estate, wherever he was at the time. Physically, he never did anything more than to massage and kiss her feet.

Thiele soon discovered this was the only harmless thing about him. She was subjected to lectures about how childish her people were for preserving outdated and impractical ideas; how they should not spread such ideas around; how only fools would render compassionate care to others; how gullible they were in negotiating agreements between parties. More subtle but no less annoying were his attempts to convert her to the Veen faction's beliefs. Thiele had always managed to get through her visits by keeping her thoughts and feelings to herself, allowing Valad to satisfy his obsession. Eventually, he would let her go.

This last time, though, had been too much for her. Prisoners had been brought to him while was at his southern estate. Valad brought her to the pens and proudly showed them off: sad-faced, wretched beings; some quiet, some pleading and hysterical. Their only crime was they opposed the policy of the Crowns. Thiele rigidly shielded her disgust and tried not to look at the marks that showed the abuse of Valad's men.

When Valad brought her back to his rooms, he proposed a pairing between them, sensing—and who wouldn't?—Thiele was nearing the time she could conceive. Thiele told him she'd think it over, then slipped out stealthily. Valad had guards out to prevent her escape, but he reckoned without knowledge of Thiele's mental abilities.

Now she and Leah were both in danger from him: Thiele of being Valad's kept mate; Leah of whatever fate Valad had in store for such prisoners. If they were captured, it would be difficult to tell whose situation would be more terrible.

Leah shuddered. Thiele realized that Leah had not been asleep, but had followed her mental pictures. Thiele frequently thought in images, particularly when remembering something. Leah undoubtedly had little trouble interpreting them. Thiele broadcast soothing feelings and conjured up a fantasy of herself and Leah tying Valad to a tree. Leah relaxed a little, seemingly reassured.

Thiele kept her foreboding to herself.

PURSUIT

She was gone.

Matvar knew the instant he awoke. Cursing, he reached for his boots and sent a command lashing out at Arunesh, who was in the common room chatting with one of the maids.

Matvar was not a heavy sleeper. He ought to have wakened as soon as she made an attempt to escape, so much did his mind resonate to hers. But he had not. He had even slept past his waking time, something he had not done since he was a boy. There was a drift of strangeness in his mind, like the aftertaste of a dream, faintly sweet, seductive, alien.

It was more than a suspicion, then. He had been caused to oversleep himself. Someone had tampered with his mind, drawn him down to the deep levels so that he would not feel the twintouch. Surely she could not have done it. She could scarcely communicate. She was like an infant. He had put her to sleep with a touch.

He reached out, frantically, as far as his rusty twin-sense could span. Was there a faint echo to the northwest? Impossible! She could not have gone so far in a night. The touch was days away.

Then he remembered the weakness of her emanations. He and his men had not even detected her existence until just before they had seen her at the wreck. Even he had not discovered the obscene mental resonance between her and himself until he had looked into her eyes. Perhaps she was not far away at all. But the sense of her, if it truly was her, was faint and blurred. There was no time to be lost.

All of these thoughts happened in less than the time it took for Arunesh to dash up the corridor and scratch at the door. Matvar was booted, on his feet, ready to receive him. "Enter!" he growled.

Arunesh opened the door and saluted. Matvar barely glanced at his second. So far no one had discovered the secret of his rapport with the Sky Dweller woman. In spite of this emergency, he must not give himself away.

"Have the men ready for inspection in half a kroon," he said. "I will see the Sky Dweller now. Go."

"Yes, my lord!" Arunesh turned smartly and strode back toward the common room. Matvar heard him stir them up. He was exceedingly proud of his promotion, was Arunesh. A good lad, well-trained, but there was a softness in him. He would never be more than second in command.

Matvar left the room, pulling on his gloves and carrying his helmet. He turned to the right and followed the corridor around the corner into the wing of the inn. The guard stood straight and still in front of the door of the secured room. There was an alert expression on his face, but his eyes stared blankly at the wall opposite. They did not move as Matvar walked up to him. The guard was not aware of his presence.

Matvar regarded him for a short moment, tapping the handle of his whip. He did not need to open the door to know that the room was empty. She was truly gone. And she was getting farther away all the time. This man, the guard, did not know she was gone. He did not even know, at that moment, of his own existence.

Who is it, Matvar wondered. Who has done this? It is a skill I have not seen before. Who? Not the Sky Dweller. She hasn't the strength. Unless....

A new, cold thought came to him. He did not really know what a Sky Dweller could or could not do. The Teachings made them powerful beings, with motives and talents far beyond the knowledge of his people. He remembered her surprising blast of emotion when Labek killed the jeweled creature, her rousing from what should have been unconsciousness. She might have been dissembling other times: the weak emanations, the suppression of her conscious levels after he touched her sleep lock, all of it.

He cleared his throat. "Soldier, open the door," he commanded.

The guard blinked. He saluted crisply, as if he had been aware of his commander's presence all along. There was no confusion. He had been gone; suddenly he was there again, without any awareness that he had been unconscious. He did not know he had been interfered with. There were no images of the alien woman in his mind, no memory of the night except having stood outside that door, of having done his duty.

He briskly unlocked the door of the room and stood aside for Matvar to enter. But Matvar stood back, arms folded, and pressed the man to go in ahead of him. The guard moved two paces into the room and stopped abruptly. His surprise was profound.

"She is not here," he said, shaking his head as if to deny the evidence of his eyes and mindsense.

Matvar examined the seals on the single window. It had not been opened. At his scowl, the guard's face began to tremble.

Arunesh came into the room with four of the men behind him. The four took the guard away, still shaking his head.

"My lord?" ventured Arunesh.

"Find out," said Matvar, "if any of the guests left the inn last night or earlier this morning. Find out who is missing and cannot be accounted for. Report on the insect creature."

"The body of the creature is secure, my lord. It is, uh, beginning to decompose. The guards moved it from the stable to a walled garden some time ago. They are watching it from a distance. Several of the inn people saw it last night, but they have been cautioned."

"So. Carry on."

"My lord."

Matvar strolled into the common room of the inn and flicked a hand at the proprietor. The man bustled forth to set the commander's food on the table of greatest honor. The serving maids who had been hanging about when

Arunesh was in command of the room melted quietly out the service doors, and the soldiers took on a busier appearance.

Matvar forced himself to eat as he reached out again for that faint presence. It was very weak but seemed no farther away. He must get her back. His future depended on it. His faith required it.

He considered. There was no way to avoid gossip. The men were under orders not to reveal the connection between the alien female and the wreck by the river. He had cunningly put the Learned One off the scent by hinting that the person in custody was a throwback, merely deformed.

Still, too many people had seen the fire in the sky two nights before. The guide had been silenced, but he was only one of a number who had seen the Star Ship for themselves. The traditions of the Old Faith were well remembered out here in the back country even if the practices were corrupted by rural ignorance. Soon, more and more people would begin seeing twinship between the ruined vessel and the strange woman.

There would be talk. It was too late to stop it entirely, but Matvar must take steps to contain the damage. He had three priorities. He must recover the Starborn. He must transport her as soon as possible to the cathedral palace in Oshune. And he must take pains to see that the credit for success would go to himself above all.

His greatest danger was the Veen. Here in the back country, their power was still small. Unfortunately, the Star Ship had had the perversity to smash itself on a province governed by a particularly unprincipled younger son of the most objectionable Veen family. Valad the Creep, Labek called him.

Matvar was prepared at this moment to forgive Valad his perversions, known and unknown. He was willing to overlook the man's insinuating, insulting manner and juvenile sense of humor. What he could not pardon, in the present situation, was Valad's undeniable intelligence. He would make twins of the evidence in no time and show his nasty face before two more nights passed.

The best course of action would be to send Arunesh with a small party of men to track the woman while Matvar remained with the rest of the troop to carry on with the patrol and keep things as quiet as possible. And to deal with Valad when he made his inevitable appearance.

However, Arunesh did not have Matvar's secret edge in locating the quarry. He would have to remain behind while Matvar took the pursuit. It was a bad business. Valad would make short work of the lieutenant, but that was not as bad as letting the Sky Dweller escape. There was not really any choice.

Arunesh came and stood respectfully before him, the innkeeper groveling in the background.

"My lord, the Learned One cannot be found. She is the only person known to be at the inn or in the village last night who cannot be accounted for."

Matvar nodded, with flattened emanations and unchanged expression. The Learned One. Could it be? They did not interfere, those odd wandering people. It was their reputation to be trustworthy and to avoid having anything to do with soldiers of the Double Crown. It was widely supposed they were some kind of religious order connected with the Old Faith, but since they were never seen to take part in its observances, their real beliefs remained vague.

"Did she pay her bill?" Matvar inquired.

"Last night, before she retired."

"She was expecting to leave early, then."

"So he thought." Arunesh gestured with his chin toward the kneeling landlord.

Matvar smoothed one glove. "Have the Learned One found," he said after a moment. "Even if she has nothing to do with the disappearance of our...of the person in our protection, she may have seen something. Have her found."

He then acquainted Arunesh with his intentions, ignoring the man's evident surprise at being left to hold command of the body of the troop. The proprietor of the inn, realizing that he was not to be held accountable for the disappearance of the very peculiar guest under guard, backed thankfully out of their presence. Matvar made a note to have a word with the man before he set out and remind him of the consequences of allowing a lot of loose talk to spread from the inn.

At mid-afternoon, the search party entered a small hamlet that straggled against the walls of a large estate. People peered at them out of doorways, and children were called in from playing. It was too early in the season for the planting; the whole population was still close to home.

Matvar felt more weary than he ought to. At least twice since midday, he had almost fallen asleep riding. He knew it was an effect of the interference in his sleep the night before, and this angered him. Dreams of Rudvar depressed him. He reached repeatedly for the emanations of the Starborn, but there was little to reassure him. He was confident of having come more or less the right direction, but she did not seem much nearer. It was disturbingly like following the dead.

He shifted in his saddle and looked around him. The fear in the eyes of the people bored him beyond expression. "I want to see the head man!" he called out.

A robust, purple individual stepped away from one of the hovels and knelt in the road before Matvar.

"I am the head man, your Honor," he said. "How may we serve you?"

"I require information. Did you or any of these people see a stranger traveling in this district, a tall, badly deformed female with feeble emanations? Has anyone heard of this person?"

"I will inquire, your Honor."

There was a buzzing among the people. Matvar felt the shimmer of the village rapport, the flying thought-symbols that served for a private language in the tiny community. Being outside their network, he gleaned little meaning from their communication. He could only project his remembered image of the alien for them to recognize or not.

They were interested; they were curious. But they had not seen her. The head man confirmed this.

"Where does this road go?" Matvar asked.

"East, your honor. After the river crossing, it turns."

"It goes nowhere," said a voice from the left.

Matvar turned. The gate in the estate wall was open. A pale blue-gray man stood there, caressing the jeweled handle of his whip. He wore high-heeled boots of gaudy design. Two pairs of bodyguards in armor made a square formation around him. It was years since Matvar had seen Valad, but he recognized him at once. Valad had not improved. The village people were suddenly out of sight.

"Magistrate," Matvar acknowledged with a slight nod.

"Commander." Valad returned the greeting with the identical tone of voice and inclination of the head.

Matvar knew he was being mocked, but he had been expecting it and kept his face and emanations smooth. He waited.

"You impress me, Commander," said Valad, eyeing Matvar's feet. "I have heard such things about your accomplishments in the short time you have been among us. I never dreamed you managed it with only four men."

"I am honored by this meeting, Magistrate," Matvar said, ignoring the comment. "I am on Crowns business and may not delay here."

"Yes, pursuing a fugitive. I heard. This interests me very much. After all, Crowns business is my business here, as you know, Commander."

"You will receive a report when time permits, Magistrate."

Valad smiled. "I detain you, do I not? Very well. Run along and do your duty, Commander. Catch her. And then bring her to me."

Matvar did not answer. He sketched a gesture of respectful departure and sent a direction to his men. The five of them turned their beasts toward the river.

Valad uttered a low chuckle. "Good hunting, Commander. I look forward to your return. I have not yet had the opportunity to offer you my hospitality. My entertainments are quite remarkable for such a wilderness, you will see. And I shall give you an introduction to my bootmaker."

His laughter followed them out of the village.

THE JOURNEY NORTH

Beast jerked to a stop. Leah awakened from her doze. Thiele dismounted ahead of her to lead Beast off the road. A stream ran at the bottom of a shallow slope. Leah noticed a bridge to her right. Beast stopped at the edge of the water to drink. Thiele took a water bottle from a saddle hook, knelt, and dipped it in a small pool near the bank. She replaced the stopper and put the bottle back on the hook.

Thiele held up her arms to Leah, inviting her to dismount. Leah slid off awkwardly. Thiele steadied her as her feet touched ground. She walked around, easing the stiffness in her legs. As she rubbed her calves, she noticed there were two, no, three, shadows at various angles. Looking up, she saw the three moons. All the moons of Autumn World orbited on a plane, so the moons appeared to move within a narrow band in the sky. The largest, the yellowish one—the one with the space station—was brighter than Earth's moon. It cast the most distinct shadow. Another moon was a dim button. Leah watched as it moved—compared to it, the other two were standing still. The smallest appeared to be a shiny jewel, no doubt due to its icy surface. Leah turned slowly, scanning the rest of the sky for a bright, moving point of light not within the band. This is how a rescue ship would appear if one were searching for her. She saw nothing but background constellations and the Milky Way.

Leah rubbed the back of her neck. Beast grazed on plants beside the river. The color was indistinct in the bright moonlight, but Leah could make out feathery leaves. Turning around, Leah saw Thiele sitting with her back against the trunk of a tree at the top of the slope, eyes closed.

Thiele's eyes opened when Leah approached. Leah's attention had turned to the tree with its scaly bark. She saw no leaves, but there seemed to be flowers on the lower branches. When the breeze blew, a sweet fragrance came from them.

In Leah's mind was a picture of how the tree—or "chatolpa," as the mental pseudo-sound came into her mind—appeared by day. It stood about 20 meters high. The flowers were orange. Leah heard cooing sounds. Looking up, she saw a bird perched at the top of a nearby tree. "Sakeret," Thiele said in her mind. She provided an image of the bird tearing at the meat of a dead animal. Beast made a grumbling sound. Leah pivoted to see a fox-like creature drinking at the stream a few meters from Beast. "Fox." Thiele repeated Leah's word telepathically, then, "fossa," identifying the small, striped animal. Beast grumbled louder; the fossa padded away. Satisfied, Beast ambled up to Thiele. He bent down for Thiele to scratch his camel-like head.

Thiele stood. Pointing to herself, then the road, she said, "We go now." Leah smiled before repeating the words. She was certain Thiele understood she was receptive to learning the spoken language.

After Thiele had pushed Leah up again, she climbed back into the saddle, and they were on their way. At first, Leah tried to take in the scenery. Trees, shrubbery, and grasses grew right up to the side of the road. Once in a while, there was an open space and the silhouette of a structure with bilateral symmetry. Leah presumed they were passing fields and farmhouses. Thiele confirmed this presumption telepathically. A few times, she thought she saw small, gopher-like creatures pause at the side of the road, only to run away as Beast passed. "Chumpers," was Thiele's pseudo-sound for them. Once, a creature the size of a deer sprang across Beast's path—since there was no danger of collision, Beast did not break stride. Leah suspected Thiele had contact with Beast's mind at some level, preventing him from shying at such things.

Not long after they had gone back on the road, Leah was again lulled into a doze. She did not know how much time had passed when Beast changed his pace. Leah saw they were not on the road anymore but on a dirt path that led into the forest. Soon she saw a clearing, and in the clearing, two buildings. When they reached a space between them, Beast stopped.

The two women dismounted. Thiele led Beast into a three-sided building with a thatched roof. She tied his reins to a wooden rail and removed the packs, found an item on a hook on one wall which appeared to be a brush with long bristles, and hastily groomed Beast. She gave Beast's reins a final tug to be certain they were securely tied, then walked to the other building. Leah followed.

The other building seemed to be a dark wooden structure of one floor. The box-like shape had a double door in the middle of the front and two double shuttered windows on each side: bilateral symmetry again, Leah thought.

Leah stood in the doorway, her eyes adjusting to the dimmer light inside. She could not see Thiele at first. Soon, though, she heard the sound of wood grating on wood as Thiele threw open the shutters. Once the windows on the other side were also open, there was enough moonlight to dimly see inside.

It was a small, one-room shack. The only piece of furniture was a wooden table. On the opposite wall stood a double fireplace with a stack of kindling beside it. Because of the neat woodpile and the lack of dust, Leah concluded Thiele had used the shack before, and recently. Thiele confirmed this telepathically as she laid the wood on the stone for burning, and lit the fire with a metal device much like one Leah had used in grammar school to light Bunsen burners.

As Thiele coaxed the sparks into flame, Leah took a long look at her. She had purple-brown skin and short brown hair. The hair was arranged in fanned-out tufts at either side of her head. Leah assumed that must be personal fashion, since she couldn't recall seeing that hair style on others. The hair tapered in the back and went down the spinal column as far as Leah could see. The slight bulge under Thiele's shirt seemed to indicate the hair went all the way to the base of the spine.

Thiele had low brows, which Leah had seen on everyone else on the planet. The thick nose and prominent ears, Leah guessed, were also species-related; however, Leah suspected that the indentation along the side of the nose and part of the cheek was due to injury. Thiele provided an image of herself falling among rocks at a shoreline. Thiele's skin was generally smooth and even-colored, indicating youth or a lot of time spent indoors, probably the former, if her familiarity with the road was any indication. For clothes, she wore boots, dark green baggy pants of a thick material secured by a macramé-type belt. Her shirt was made of the same material but more of an olive green. Over all she had worn a loose purple-black coat that came to her knees. It was now folded on the floor beside her. The coat had no buttons or fasteners of any sort. It was lined with a fuzzy, dark orange material.

Thiele brushed dust and ash from her hands and stood. Now that the fire was blazing brightly, she shut the windows and doors. Leah saw there was no glass in the windows—only an opening covered by shutters. Turning to look at the rest of the room, Leah noticed cabinets along the walls at her left and right. A glint from a cabinet shelf caused her to walk over to inspect it. Inlaid on the counter top was something that looked like part of a circuit board. It was not connected to anything here—it seemed to be merely a patch in a broken surface. Leah gasped and stared. She turned to Thiele.

"Things like that can be found all around here," Thiele said, using images to convey the meaning. "People pick them up and use them for whatever they can."

Leah caught the meaning. She tried to concentrate on this surprising information. Remembering Thiele's fragment of a circuit board and images of space travel, she wondered whether these people had traveled in space. No, that didn't follow. It was a long way from circuit boards and dreams of space travel to the technology of space travel. It was too difficult to think out. She was too tired. She set it aside for later and stood looking quietly at the room around her.

She ran her hand along the surface of the counter. It was smooth with sanding, or long use, or both. She noticed that black was the wood's natural color, not paint or stain. Black and gray boards were on the floor and walls as well. Looking up, she saw the same material had been used in the ceiling beams.

Meanwhile, Thiele rolled out a thick blanket or sleeping bag on the floor. "You sleep here," she said to Leah, with an image of her wrapped in the blanket, sleeping.

"Where will you sleep?" asked Leah.

In answer, Thiele put a hand on the lapel of her coat and shook it. She sent Leah an image of herself sleeping by the fire wrapped in it.

Leah's first instinct was to protest, but a phrase such as "Oh, you shouldn't," was too abstract in word and thought—or else, Thiele pretended not to understand. She patted the blanket invitingly. Leah's training took over: she had been instructed not to refuse another being's hospitality unless physically or ethically impossible. She walked over and lay on the blanket.

She expected Thiele to lie down as well. Instead, Thiele walked to the table, where she had laid her packs, and took out two small, metal bowls. She walked out after sending Leah an image of a pool. Was Thiele going to take a bath?

It seemed a long time before Thiele returned. Leah heard footsteps outside. She wondered what she ought to do if it wasn't Thiele. But Thiele walked in, a bowl in each hand. She used a foot to ease the doors shut again. After placing both bowls on the floor in front of Leah, she went back and threw a wooden bolt across the doors.

Thiele knelt in front of Leah. She offered one bowl to Leah with a gesture. Leah dipped a finger in and tasted it, to Thiele's apparent amazement. It was water. Thiele walked to her pack and retrieved a metal cup. She poured the water into it and gave it to Leah. Suddenly thirsty, Leah drank. As she did, Thiele dipped a cloth in the bowl and proceeded to wash her face and hands. Leah felt like a fool. With all of her own water gone, she couldn't imitate the gesture. What would Thiele think? Had she ruined some ritual?

Apparently sensing Leah's distress, Thiele lay so that her head was at Leah's level. Slowly, she reached out and stroked Leah's side, sending out the same soothing thought impressions she had sent at the inn. She clasped Leah's hand firmly.

"Friend," she said. The accompanying thought impression gave Leah no doubt about the meaning.

When Thiele awoke, Leah was still asleep. That didn't surprise her since Leah seemed to have a sick headache all along.

Thiele went outside to the rude stable. She filled a trough for Beast from the rain barrel and cut some firn with her long knife for his manger. After brushing him down thoroughly, she went inside.

Leah hadn't moved. Thiele took a clean cloth from her pack and spread it on the table. She placed food on it, mostly leftovers from last night's dinner: hard bread, white cheese, assorted dried vegetables. Thinking to make a little vegetable broth, she took a bucket, went outdoors to the brook, and rinsed and filled the bucket. The rivers and streams had long since been washed clean of industrial pollution; outside the cities, they ran clear and fresh.

She had nearly reached the hut when the rustling of brush made her stop and turn. Thiele froze. There, not far away, were insects she had glimpsed in Leah's mind while they were in telepathic contact. These weren't the tiny creatures Thiele had thought they were. They were as tall as Thiele's knee and maybe twice, three times as long. They glimmered in the sunlight, antennae and forelegs and mandibles moving restlessly. The mandibles looked as if they could deliver a cruel bite. Slowly, Thiele inched her way to the cottage door. She closed it behind her in relief and put down the bucket.

Apparently sensitive to Thiele's distress, Leah woke. There was a concerned questioning note to her thoughts. Thiele sent the image of the green insects. Immediately, Leah brushed past her and walked outside. Thiele followed.

The insects hadn't moved. Leah talked to them, beckoning to them. Thiele matched words with images to learn a little more of Leah's language. She concluded Leah was trying to get the insects to come to her. They rotated in their position so that they faced Leah, but that was all. Leah tried for a good long while to entice them to come. She moved forward to try to touch them. They backed away and scurried into the woods. Leah put her hands down and sighed.

Thiele went back into the cottage. She took the pot off the fireplace hook, rinsed it, put water back in, and turned the arm inside the fire for the water to boil. At the table she set about cleaning and chopping vegetables.

Leah didn't come back right away. Thiele guessed that she went to wash or to relieve herself. Eventually Thiele heard splashing. Craning her neck, she peered through the window she had opened earlier. Leah was washing in the rain barrel. She walked in as Thiele pulled the pot over to dump the vegetable cubes in. Thiele put the pot back on the fire and pointed to the table. "Breakfast. Food. Eat," she said, with appropriate mental images.

Leah examined the food closely, turning each item in her hand, sniffing at it. When she had gone through all the pieces, she sat heavily on the floor. Thiele caught the image of a being like Leah in a purple dress taking a bite out of a red spherical thing and collapsing to the ground. Then the figure lay prone in a transparent container surrounded by seven smaller beings of her kind. Through it all, Thiele caught the central message: is this food poison to me? But there was an even stronger impression: so *hungry*. The urge was so strong in Leah that Thiele's own appetite increased. She broke the bread and ate half of it greedily. When she offered the other half to Leah, Leah tore off a bite, put it in her mouth, let it linger for a little while, then swallowed.

Thiele rinsed her own travel mug and the spare that she'd offered to Leah the night before, then filled them with water. Leah drank eagerly. Then she tried a bite of each of the vegetables the way she did the bread. Some pieces she spat out and threw into the hearth, deliberately wide of the pot.

When Thiele deemed the stew was ready, she dipped her mug into it. She indicated to Leah to do the same, but Leah only took enough broth to cover the bottom of her mug. She avoided the vegetable pieces. She drank, filled her mug again from the water bucket, and drank some more. After that, Thiele could not coax her to eat more. Thiele ate quickly herself and put the leftovers back in her pack.

Leah sat by the fire. Thiele settled herself nearby with her back resting against a wall, thinking. Now that she had the leisure, she had to consider what to do next. Beast could carry two, but it was slower travel than with one. There were others of Leah's people on the moon—Leah thought of them often—so Thiele knew it was more important than ever to get the electronic parts back home quickly to facilitate contact.

They had been lucky so far; they had not met anyone else, but in the long journey home, by road or by forest, it was inevitable they'd meet someone. When they did, how was Thiele to explain Leah or keep her from harm if they were attacked? Alone, Thiele could take care of herself, but she was a scholar and a diplomat, not a soldier, not skilled in the fighting arts.

Leah seemed to be picking up the images that accompanied Thiele's reasoning. "I stay here?" she asked.

"No," said Thiele. Leah understood the negative. Thiele pictured the shack. It could not be seen from the road but might be found if a search pattern was instituted. Also, Leah's telepathic emanations—however weak— might draw searchers to her. Further, there was no food stored here, and Leah did not know how to look for edible plants, or even what to look for. Nor could she yet communicate easily with strangers.

Thiele considered pairing Leah with another traveler from home. Sesse and Nitcha were supposed to be in this area, but handing Leah to one of them would simply be giving them the problem, not solving it. She did, though, have friends who lived in the area. Closest by was a woman, an eccentric, who lived by herself, deeper in the forest. She was unlikely to be visited by searchers, and even if she was, she could hide Leah effectively. In the meantime, Thiele could go home and try to contact Leah's people.

Leah stared at her intensely, following her thoughts. In Leah's mind was a picture of Beast tripping and Thiele falling to the ground. The implied question: what happens to me if something happens to you?

Thiele considered that. It was a good point: if Thiele were injured or killed on the way back, who would know of Leah? Who would help her? The old woman would help Leah at her home but was unlikely to go on a journey on her behalf. Thiele sat back and concentrated. Slowly, another plan came to her mind. There were three others, friends, who lived in a rough line between here and Thiele's home. Each was opposed to the ruling government, though secretly. Each could take and hide Leah temporarily. Each could move Leah to the next house, if necessary, whatever happened to Thiele in the meantime.

Leah, reading the map and method in Thiele's mind, seemed to approve. In Leah's thoughts was a hazy analogy of a similar transport method she knew of. "Yes, do," she said.

Thiele stood. She put a hand on Leah's arm while sending an affirming thought. She gathered the pots and mugs to go to the stream and wash them out in preparation for the next leg of the journey.

When Thiele had gone, Leah's mind turned to her friends, Topaz and Diamond. What of them? Where were they? Should she go and look for them? No, she decided, better not. With no idea where they were, her chances of finding them were very small, as painful as that was to admit. The best chance of her survival and theirs was for her or Thiele to get to a radio and contact the base to ask for a rescue team.

She stood, brushed off her pants, and walked outside. In the shed, Beast placidly munched on vegetation. Leah stroked his side. At first, Beast tolerated the touch, but then he shook her hand off with a grumble of protest. Puzzled, Leah backed away. She heard sounds outside. She thought she recognized a buzz in her head that meant *someone else nearby.* Assuming it was Thiele, Leah walked out.

In the space between her and the shack, Leah saw four beings of Thiele's species staring at her. Their clothes were in rags, patched in places, torn in others. Three were about Thiele's height; one was small and had a finger in his mouth. Whether it was from their appearance or whether she was receiving impressions of intention, Leah felt threatened. Without a word, they slowly separated and surrounded her. Leah felt a sudden painful hunger—were these people starving? It might be so, she thought, for she could almost see the skeletal structure of their heads and hands under the skin. She held out her hands, palms open, to show them she had no food. From the shed, Beast grumbled more loudly. He apparently sensed danger, too.

Surely, thought Leah, when they see I have nothing, they will leave me alone? But they inched closer. Leah turned slowly, hands still out, but it did not seem to daunt them. What was she to do? Leah could fight, but the damned gravity was so strong, the atmosphere so thick, she couldn't walk upright without feeling she was moving through water. To take on four at once was risky enough under normal circumstances. It would be impossible under these conditions.

They were almost within arm's reach now. Would they hurt her? Surely they could see she had nothing they could eat. Would they think of eating *her?* Desperately, awkwardly, she tried to project the thought: I have nothing you want. I come in peace. Please leave me alone.

In answer, she got the overwhelming impression that they wanted her watch. The wristband was highly polished metal. Perhaps that was valuable in this low-industrial society. Moving slowly, turning slowly, she took the watch off and held it out to them. Gingerly, one of the adults took it, and stepped back quickly. All remained in arm's reach.

They seemed to be holding a conference. Maybe they'll take the watch and go away, she thought. I hope that's all they want. The adult with the watch put it in a battered pocket.

Leah turned, startled, to see the child pluck her sleeve. An adult knelt, reached over, and tugged at her pants. Oh, no, they want my clothes, too, she thought. What do I do now? If only Thiele would come back. Yes, that's it, she thought. Shout, and try to shout mentally, as well. But as she gathered herself for the effort, another adult pulled out a knife and the effort was wasted in a gasp.

Thiele could sense something was wrong a long way off. She stopped rinsing utensils immediately and ran for the cottage. As she ran, she saw the two green insects run from the cover of the brush in front of her toward Beast's stable. When she turned the corner, she saw in the space between the house and shed a group of four people with Leah on the bottom, the insects on top. The insects were clicking their mandibles, biting Leah's attackers.

Thiele stood still, silently, for a few moments, gathering her strength. Then she let out a great mental shout. The four attackers staggered away, holding their heads, but Leah caught the force of it, too. The insects merely scrambled aside, apparently confused.

Avoiding the insects, Thiele walked to Leah and knelt beside her. Before she could do anything, she sensed the attackers waiting at the edge of the clearing. They were planning to return when their heads stopped reverberating. Thiele gathered her wits again, got a good grip on Leah's shoulder, and sent a mental command: run!

They did. So did the insects. Leah also caught the impulse again, but because of her own slow movements and Thiele's grip, she did little more than struggle to her knees. Thiele took Leah's face in her hands and soothed the worst of the telepathic discomfort. But there was a pain in her arm. She put her hands down and examined her own arm, puzzled. There was no bruise or cut. Then it occurred to her that she had felt Leah's pain while in close contact with her mind. Sure enough, there was a gash in Leah's arm, behind the elbow.

"Wiggle your fingers." Thiele demonstrated her words.

Leah complied slowly. Good; no tendons cut, no major injury.

"Come, I'll wash and bind it." Thiele helped Leah to her feet.

As Thiele dressed the wound, she said, "We can't stay here long. They know where the shack is. They might come back."

Leah understood the thought impressions, if not the words. "Yes. I'm afraid we've lost Diamond and Topaz again."

Thiele nodded, comprehending the association of names to insects. "I can't take you to my friend, as I'd planned. You're hurt. It's too far." She showed a map in her mind and a house with her friend standing in front of it. "I'll have to take you to Akashtai, the old woman, instead." Thiele again pinpointed the area on her mental map along with the image of the old woman and her dwelling place. "She can help you. Later, maybe, you can find your way to my friend, or I can return to you." Thiele sent the appropriate images.

Leah seemed to understand, despite her pain. Thiele gathered her things. Leah remained in the shack while Thiele fetched the pots and saddled Beast. She came back for Leah and pushed her onto Beast's saddle. When they were on their way, Leah secure in the saddle, Thiele lulled her to sleep. It was the only way she could think of to ease her pain. Then she reinforced the mental image of the house she'd originally planned to take Leah to and how to get there. Thiele would stop there and explain the situation on her way home in case Leah arrived there later.

As Beast settled into his traveling stride, Thiele scanned around them for any sign of the bandits or others who might be following. There were none.

JUMPER FRIEND

Jumper-friend faced the Western Sky, leaping, dancing furiously. In a short while, the sunset would begin. She must draw the great globe out of the sky into his own cave and coax the guardians into the night sky.

Her dance froze abruptly, like leaves suddenly grown quiet in the eye of a storm. Someone approached from the east. Not her own people, who rarely came to her Deep Woods cave to seek her. Perhaps one of those her people called the Learned Ones—those whom she thought of as the Northfolk. (She had read the cold images in their minds: one thought the sibilant speech of Jumper-friend's people sounded like new crystalline snow brushing across brittle mats of frozen wirethorn on the northern flats.)

Jumper-friend puzzled what to do. She felt the need to investigate the strangers. She needed to bring night upon the world. Finally, with resolve, she danced, setting the ancient patterns into motion, traveling silently from the sacred ground toward the east. The guardians would rise tonight, spilling their triple brilliance across the night skies.

Jumper-friend approached the sounds and took refuge behind a stray stand of golden lace. The newly-leafing trees provided too little cover. She watched two figures arriving with their riding beast. One rode, one led.

The one leading she knew. One of the Northfolk who often came this way, who had stayed in the village of Jumper-friend's people before.

The one who rode was like no creature Jumper-friend had ever seen. She was a person, as the Jumpers were people. Of that Jumper-friend was almost certain. Yet she stood tall and frail as a sapling. Her coloring recalled the sight of a piece of bark falling from the limbs of a bheshwood-tree.

The creature—Leah, the creature supplied as a name—appeared to be injured. One arm was swathed in torn cloth, the cloth itself colored with blood thick and dark as rhizo.

When the Learned One turned to speak to the stranger, Jumper-friend took the opportunity to walk out into the open unobserved. The Northerner Thiele looked back to find Jumper-friend there and went to greet her. "Akashtai—friend of the Jumpers," she hailed the older woman, extending her hands. Thiele found the name amusing, for she did not believe Jumpers existed, but she used it out of courtesy for the eccentric healer's choice. She took a deep breath and said, "Akashtai, this child is from a far-off land. She is injured and needs healing."

"She fell from the sky," Jumper-friend said confidently.

Thiele looked uncomfortable. "That must not be said to one and all. There are those who would kill the Sky Dweller. Will she—will Leah—be safe in your care? And can you heal her?"

Jumper-friend considered this carefully. "She will be safe in my care. I do not know if I can heal her. Having never seen one of these mended, how can I be sure what to do when it is broken? If I can learn her differences—and if she is meant to receive healing—then I will heal her."

Thiele nodded. She could do nothing more. "She is not from this world, Akashtai. She did fall from the sky. On our world, some of life is poisonous to her, some foods. Take care what you feed her or use to heal her."

Jumper-friend rocked back on her heels, studying the Leah-creature with interest. Thiele continued, "When she is strong enough to travel, she will go to a friend's house." Thiele bent to draw a map in the soil with her finger. She explained the route north, the three safe houses. She sent mental images of the route to Akashtai's mind to reinforce the drawing. "I will attempt to return for her along this route, but if she is well, she must not wait. She must begin the journey on her own." Thiele wiped the map away and stood up. "Perhaps you could find someone reliable to escort her? The Veen will want to lay hands on her. and there are many other dangers she could come to."

Jumper-friend studied the alien. "It will be as you say. She will come to the first house safely." Jumper-friend looked to the sky and saw with relief that her dances had worked even far from the sacred ground: the sun was setting.

Thiele followed the line of her gaze. "I must leave soon. Someone may be following me, and it would be best to travel by night."

Thiele went back to her ornit and helped Leah down. As she redistributed her packs and prepared to ride out again, she quietly explained to Leah the arrangements she had made with Akashtai.

Jumper-friend left the two to their conversation for the moment and walked east toward the woods from which they had come. Tentatively, she searched for the mind of her granddaughter, the last child of one of the third set of twins. The girl's mind was easy to distinguish among the others, a singling consciousness as was Akashtai's own now.

Jumper-friend called the child to her, sending images of a journey north, of danger and adventure. She knew what happened tonight and tomorrow would not be duplicated again in the whole of Ashven's world. If this singlet child was to dance the guardians into the night sky long after Jumper-friend had slipped beyond Ashven's Veil, then it could only increase her power to witness this.

Thiele was ready to leave. Jumper-friend heard her saying her farewell to Leah. Thiele turned her beast and rode to Jumper-friend. "Thank you for accepting this burden, Akashtai. Heal her if you can. Send her to me safe."

Jumper-friend bowed her head for one moment, then looked into Thiele's eyes. "I have said it. It will be so."

Thiele glanced back at Leah briefly, then set her ornit on its way back into the forest.

Jumper-friend turned to her new charge. She sent images of warmth, food, rest. The being agreed tiredly and rose to follow Jumper-friend to the cave she had pictured.

Jumper-friend sat Leah near her hearth and set out to build the embers into a blaze. She pulled her cookpot onto the fire and poured water from a corked jug into it. Then she turned to the alien's wounds. She unwrapped the makeshift bandages and studied the gash in the woman's thin upper arm.

Why was this one so thin? Was she already diseased before she was injured? Jumper-friend pinched the being's other arm. Leah made a small sound of protest but did not move. The muscles appeared to be atrophied. Jumper-friend concluded that the pink around the wound must be a healthy sign, for she had seen the same color in the other arm when the blood rushed to the skin where she pinched it.

Jumper-friend scooped some of the boiling water into a basin, some of it into a jug she used for tea. Then she tossed the bandages into what remained of the water in the cooking pot. She would let them boil for awhile.

Jumper-friend made a tea that should help the body replace the lost blood quickly. At least, that was what it did in her own people. She was not sure what it would do to the alien. Somehow the blood loss and the being's tiredness seemed far more dangerous than the wound itself. Jumper-friend had to risk that the tea she handed to Leah would help.

Leah accepted the mug and sniffed at it cautiously. She took a sip and held it in her mouth. She did not seem to think it poisonous, for she swallowed it. Then she made a face. Jumper-friend caught the thought, "It certainly *tastes* like medicine." She smiled at Leah. "You must drink as much as you can. It will heal you."

Jumper-friend turned toward the cave opening as she felt her granddaughter approach. A moment later a wild mane of purple hair was shoved into the cave, followed by a smooth blue face and muscular body. The child Angin looked around. She stared at the creature by the fire and then fearlessly strode up to it. She knelt and examined it carefully.

"This is why you called? Why you were excited?"

"Yes," Jumper-friend agreed. "It is a being that fell from the sky. It was injured, and one of the Learned brought it to be healed. When it can travel, it must be taken to a house the Learned One knows. I have said it will be so."

Angin nodded, knowing a command when she heard one. "Does it speak? Is it intelligent? What is it called?"

"It calls itself Leah." Jumper-friend gestured to the alien. "Ask it your other questions yourself."

Angin turned her attention to the creature. "You are Leah?" she said aloud.

"Yes. What are you called?" The being spoke directly into her mind, and Angin was momentarily startled.

"I am Angin."

Leah cocked her head to one side, obviously puzzled. "Angin—like the river?"

Angin laughed with delight. "Yes, Angin, twin to the river. Solitary, strong, and bountiful."

It was clearly a joke, but Leah did not understand the humor. She searched for something polite to say and finally asked, "Are you the one who will take me where I need to go?"

"I am one of them. The others you will meet tomorrow, if I understand what Akashtai plans for you. You must rest now. Akashtai is thinking your wound is not serious, and you may be able to travel soon. Perhaps even tomorrow." Angin's eyes lit with excitement. "We will both need our rest. It will be a day to remember."

Jumper friend knelt beside them and gave Angin a nudge to get her moving. "Get food for supper now. It is late." Angin went to obey, and Jumper-friend quietly set to cleaning and re-bandaging Leah's arm. By the time she was done, Angin had returned with a chunk of bread and a pan filled with nuts, dried fruits, and vegetables. The three picked among them for their cold supper, and Leah obediently drank more of the medicinal tea.

Jumper-friend offered her hammock and blanket to Leah. The old woman and child curled up beneath Leah on the cave floor to sleep.

Leah arranged herself carefully, full length on the hammock, spreading her fingers to rest on the taut fabric. The brew Akashtai gave her was spreading warmth through her body, easing the throb in her arm, the ache in every muscle. She had finally filled her stomach, too, eating a good portion of those chunks of slightly pear-flavored vegetable and some of the blue bread. She had tried them both with Thiele at the hut, and they hadn't caused any problems yet, so presumably they were safe for her to eat. From Angin's mind she caught names and brief pictures of the original plants: "setony" was the vegetable, a knobbly, yellow and white thing growing on a bush; "kerm" was either the bread, or the grain from which it was made, or possibly both.... She slept.

Sometime in the night, she woke up. Things had changed. She felt different. What was it? After a moment she understood. She was healthy, well; much of her strength had returned.

A little light came from the banked embers of the fire. She could barely make out Angin and Akashtai asleep beside it. She smelled the remains of Akashtai's medicinal tea, along with other odors: something hot and spicy that might be the fire itself, scents pungent, sweet, earthy, faintly sour.

The memory of the crash nagged at her. How could it have happened? What went wrong? Was it possible some group here on-planet had known about them, watched their descent, and attacked them? Should they have waited longer to make contact with the Autumn Worlders—or tried sooner?

It had been obvious that they would want to make contact. There was a space station on the largest moon, besides their own, the remains of an earlier, unknown group of space travelers. They guessed their forerunners had been a confederation of different races, like their own, as the station seemed to be fitted out for a variety of physical types. Damage from stray comets made it hard to judge. Other groups had been sent to explore other planetary systems, to find other traces of the earlier voyagers, but so far without success. Some argued that the Autumn Worlders must have built the moon station themselves and somehow lost the technology that got them there. Leah thought again about the circuit boards she'd seen. It might fit the idea of a lost technology, but it didn't match the moon station in complexity, and it didn't match the style, either.

On Autumn World itself there were ruins that looked like places for shuttle ships to land. Erosion by air and water had left the shuttle ports in even worse shape than the moon station, but they were there. And everyone was itching to get to the surface to examine them and learn enough of the language to ask the inhabitants what they knew about them. Her boss, although Hultzu himself, had complained of the station commander's Hultzu thoroughness in making detailed observations first, by means of carefully camouflaged orbital spy modules. There was time enough for talk, the commander had said, with a nod of the head for emphasis, and her face glinted as the vestigial scales caught the light. The planet wouldn't run away, and neither would their moon. So they watched.

It had been a junior grade com tech, fooling around, who discovered someone on the planet was using amplitude modulation radio. The news had gone all over the base in no time, of course, and there were immediate demands for an answer from the base. The commander was against it, and it looked as though she was right, because as soon as the base began signaling, the on-planet radio had stopped. The decision to send an investigating mission was made, and Leah had been the sociologist assigned to it. But it was a long way from primitive radio to the type of missile that could down a shuttle.

A flaw in the shuttle? Their maintenance was painstakingly careful, but nothing was infallible.

Pilot error? But their training was painstakingly careful, too. And the pilot was dead. And she was separated from Topaz and Diamond.

So that leaves me, she thought, the junior member of this expedition, to try to find the radio people or at least survive until a rescue arrives. She wondered if Akashtai's plans would get her anywhere near a ruin. She could hardly do much investigating while eluding pursuit, and she needed more knowledge not just of the language, but of the people, before she could try badgering them with questions. She wished she could have waited quietly by the shuttle, but the crash must have been visible for kilometers, and all sorts of people would have come swarming around eventually. It was a good thing she had been able to get away from that troop of soldiers, or whatever they were. And the shock of reading their officer's mind…. It had thrown her into a confusion of emotions. Hatred and fear, longing and reverence, one of them felt some of them, at least, but she didn't know who or which. Was it the officer? But he was a native Autumn Worlder. He must be used to being a telepath. Thiele hadn't been upset.

Did Thiele come from the radio people? She seemed to know who and what Leah was—an alien—from off-world. She was neither afraid of her, nor inclined to treat her like a godling or a demon. Leah had been still half dazed then, but surely the telepathic pictures Thiele had shown her had included an operating radio? Thiele had some knowledge of what science and technology were all about even though she seemed to be a kind of wanderer herself.

For the time being, Leah thought, the best she could do was go along with Thiele's plan. If only she knew what had happened to Topaz and Diamond! They were her friends, and they were hurt, suffering over the loss of theirself. Had they gone back to the crash site? Could they find anything to eat? *Follow me!* she thought, although she knew they could not read her mind. *Follow me!—I'm going to find a radio.* With that hope, she relaxed into the curve of the hammock and went to sleep again.

When Jumper-friend returned from calling the sun to rise, Angin was already feeding Leah breakfast and tea. She handed a mug to her grandmother and turned back to her conversation with Leah. "If Akashtai says you are well enough today, we will call for the Jumpers. They can carry us to your friend's house faster than even a kurval could. Akashtai alone can call the Jumpers," Angin said proudly.

"Jumpers?" Leah picked up a brief image of something that looked vaguely like a kangaroo, but she couldn't be sure.

"They fell from the sky, as you did. Only it was many ages ago, before Akashtai was born. I think even before the Jumpers who live here now were born. Hardly anyone alive has ever seen one. I think only our people remember the old stories. But they are a friend to my grandmother and come to her when she calls them." Angin's face took on a dreamy expression and, for a moment, her dark eyes looked a little less like the eyes of a wildcat. "I have only seen them twice. There is nothing in the world that looks like them or thinks like them. Even being near them makes you glad."

Jumper-friend frowned with concern over Angin's description. How had the Jumpers so enchanted the child already? What would she be like after traveling in their presence for even a day or two?

Resolutely, she pushed the thought away. "Come, no time to talk the day away if we are to meet the Jumpers. Run to the village and bring a cart. We will need one to carry Leah. Pack food for two, for two days. Go now."

Angin ran from the cave, not bothering to conceal her excitement. Jumper-friend silently changed Leah's bandages and helped her out into the cool spring morning. It was obvious from her movements that Leah was feeling better. She stretched gingerly and wandered about, poking curiously at the vegetation. She seemed to be searching for something, but Jumper-friend could not think what.

Angin came back soon. She had obviously dressed for the journey. From the crown of her head to the small of her back, her hair was dressed in thick braids, decorated with small wooden beads. She wore leather moccasin-like shoes; dark green pants of coarse texture, gathered at the ankles; and a loose cream-colored tunic of similar cloth. The tunic had a pattern of leaves embroidered in many colors at neck, wrist, and hem. In the back, it fastened at the neck and then fell open to display the careful pattern of beaded braids along her spine. Around her neck on a narrow thong, she wore a delicate circlet of shells. She pulled a cart and produced two compactly wrapped bundles. She tied one bundle to her waist with a wide sash and then helped Leah tie hers also. Jumper-friend used a similar sash to secure Leah's arm close to the body so the jolting of the cart would not tear open the wound again.

"I have called the Jumpers. Early this morning," Jumper-friend said quietly and caught Angin's brief look of disappointment. "We will go south to meet them."

She helped Leah into the small cart—there was barely room for the tall woman to sit inside—and Angin picked up the shafts of the cart. The two women began to run, Angin pulling the cart along.

"I will leave you here," Jumper-friend said when they halted late that afternoon. "Over that hill, the Jumpers await you. "

Angin turned to lend an arm to the alien, helping her up the slope.

As Jumper-friend watched the two climb the hill and disappear over its summit, she wondered if there was perhaps something else that she should have told Angin or the Sky Dweller. She tried to project her thoughts to them as she said aloud, "Beware. The Jumpers sometimes keep that which they come to love too well." But as she picked up the shafts of the cart and turned back toward her village, she felt sure they had been too far away to receive her message.

THE BROKERS OF KNOWLEDGE

"Isolate," Koriam swore. He hadn't managed to spread the layers of metal thin enough. Or the workroom hadn't been clean enough. Or he hadn't set up the links right. Trouble was, there were too many possibilities. It looked like a silicon flake, and it smelled like one, but as far as the computer was concerned, it wasn't.

"Well, calm down," said Verret, looking up from her calculated inventories. Unlike Koriam, who liked to build things, she liked to fidget with quantities of trivia, counting and ordering, and using up what their colleagues considered an unconscionable amount of time monopolizing the computers. "Thiele may bring back plenty of silicon flakes, for all we know."

"We're a bunch of scavenging skypouncers," said Koriam, in a voice softer, but not otherwise calmer.

"Just as well," said Verret. "If we don't pick the bones, the stuff goes to metal dealers and gets made into tools that are *much* less interesting." She checked something off on the list. "*And* frequently lethal."

"We make weapons, too," said Koriam.

"Yes, remind me to argue about that next council session. But ours are more interesting, I give them that."

Koriam thought about agreeing to remind her, if she agreed to support him in his arguments, that the Philosophers should spend more time trying to build new equipment. He was tired of saying it, but what do skypouncers do when the bones are picked clean and the prey long since dead? Verret agreed, but it was just that she didn't feel the urgency of it as he did. There were good pickings still.

Koriam set down the not-a-flake with craftsman's gentleness, although he felt more like throwing it, and stomped out of the laboratory.

In the hallway beyond, he stopped aghast when he beheld one of the sound-sender operators gazing intently into the sound-pick, the equipment obviously in use. The other operator was playing dice, right hand against the left.

"What is this?" Koriam demanded.

Both operators jumped and looked at him.

"Just passing the time," said the dicer, and

"Just a little experiment," said the one at the sound-pick.

"No sound-sending, remember?" said Koriam.

"Oh!" said the one at the sound-pick, with an unawareness of wrongdoing that set Koriam's temper on edge again. But before he could complain, the youngster added, "I was trying to see if the sound-pick could act as a wand to focus thoughts in mind-speech. Some people can send further using wands.

My twin is out where I can just 'hear' him, and we're keeping track of where we lose touch."

By this time, Koriam had realized that the sound-pick was, in fact, off. He thought about apologizing verbally for his abruptness, but decided he didn't want to admit to having started to make the accusations that fortunately hadn't come out. If they'd picked up the gist of what he hadn't said, they must also be noticing that he rued it. So he only said, "Does it work?"

"Yes, but no. I mean, it focuses you all right, but it's no better than a wand."

Koriam could not help snorting. "What makes you think it would be?"

"Well—I thought it might. You don't know if you don't try."

Koriam winced at the use of the inspiring motto of the Learned and headed out without further acknowledgment. He grabbed his shawl from the rack by the door. They were high enough in the hills to feel a bite in the breeze even in good weather.

And the weather was good. Koriam wrapped the shawl around him, wriggled his shoulders to loosen tense muscles, and wandered up the slope. There was a cup where golden lace grew, waist high, with the ground at the rim covered by long, low red-eel. The eel-shaped vines were not true red in the hill variety but had a paler, darker tone, touched with gray and blue, the little round leaves almost like miniature faces. The golden lace was paler in the lowlands, too, but in the sunlight there was no obvious difference. He sat down, flattening the golden lace cushion-like beneath him. The crushed leaves would rise, gradually, after he left. Sometimes he spent more time watching the golden lace clear his traces away than he had done sitting.

Verret, who thought better indoors, had once fallen in the resin woods and sprained her ankle. At the time she fell, she was not far from the laboratory, and she had simply called for help mentally. While it was coming, she had locked onto Koriam to borrow his preference for thinking outdoors. And she had finished off some good work in the process, besides distracting herself from the pain in her ankle, but when she let go of Koriam, she started to cringe, feeling even more agoraphobic than before with the smell of the trees closing in on her, and she refused to go out again for a week after, delegating all her outdoor supervisory chores. And Koriam kept picking up her discomfort during that week, unless he stayed indoors himself (which fidgeted them both) or walked a long way to get out of range.

Here at the cup, he could still feel a buzz of activity from the rest of the community, but if he did not reach out to single an awareness from among them, the feeling was as restful as the droning of honeyseeks over the red-eels. At first he simply sat in the light, and then he started to turn over in his mind the pattern of the wells linking the levels of his silicon flake. The flaw might be in the design rather than the work. He had almost pinned down where it would be, assuming that was it, when an awareness suddenly singled itself out and became noticeable. He could not avoid noticing it. That was the curse of being Blessed. He and Palmo, his identical twin, could not help intruding on each other, if some similarity of word or visualization chimed them together. The divine quality of rapport, so welcome in most ways, and so much revered on their world, was something of a nuisance among the Learned. Indeed, Koriam had only just won election to his half of the Headship, losing support because of his built-in distractibility. On the other hand, although the motive was kept repressed and private, there were those who had voted for him because he was, after all, one of the Blessed. Which of these groups actually thought more of his abilities as a scholar was a question he had not yet unriddled to his satisfaction.

Palmo sent an apologetic greeting and started towards him, arriving at the cup later. "It's a good place," he said.

Koriam agreed, and they sat in silence for a moment, considering the colors of ground and sky. Palmo knew such things better, for his specialties were agricultural and botanical, but with Koriam he could forget their properties and concentrate on the pleasure of the sight. That enjoyment did not, however, seem sufficient in itself for Palmo's decision to join him, and Koriam at last said and thought, "Well?"

Palmo hesitated, and the blue tones of his skin flushed a little towards purple. Then he said and thought, "You're keeping the sound-senders off?"

"Of course. What do you suggest?"

"We don't have any evidence to show that whoever started broadcasting to us is hostile."

"The Two Crowns don't care much for us, and the odds are that anyone who's built a working sound-sender is either one of theirs or likely to be found by them."

"We could find out before they locate us if that's the case. Besides, who says it's likely to be a native at all? The Crowns discourage learning. New things sometimes change the old ones around too much for their liking. And how could someone find it out alone?"

"The world is full of ruins with components to loot," said Koriam. He had a picture in his head for a moment of Thiele riding towards them. Was she alone? And was it his imagination, or his twin's, or a rare moment of true far-sight? She was gone before he could decide.

Palmo had jumped to his feet and was straining mentally.

"Stop that," said Koriam, "You'll just give us a headache."

"She might be in trouble."

"If she is, she seems to be outrunning it, and we can't help."

"But—"

"Oh, sit down and finish your argument, why don't you?"

Palmo thumped down again. "If we sent out a call, we might be able to find out," he muttered.

"Maybe, but endangering all the community to check on Thiele isn't much of an argument. I'm sorry."

"Yes, I know." Palmo collected his thoughts, forcing his personal anxiety, if not out of his own mind, at least out of his brother's. "What I wanted to say—yes, I know there's enough cleverness and spare parts out there to duplicate a sound-sender, but it isn't just getting it going. There's inventing a new code—"

"What code? They're sending us prime numbers and arithmetic."

"You know perfectly well what code. Now that we know what to listen for, we've been picking up faint scraps of what they say to each other. It isn't random noise, no matter what some people like to think."

"It probably isn't," said Koriam cautiously.

"A complete code or language, all ready to use from the moment they spotted us—is it really likely?"

"A code or *language?*" Koriam echoed.

"Yes, language, it has to be," said Palmo. "It's the Starborn come back to us, and the heavens know we need the help! We should be calling them ourselves, not hiding from them."

"When did you get religion?"

"Oh, be sensible. How can you believe in a sound-sender that powerful and a code we can't break coming from the Two Crowns?"

"I'm being sensible," Koriam retorted. "If it's the Starborn, who's to say they're benevolent just because the legends say so? If there are any Starborn, they abandoned us ages gone with no thought for our welfare. We wait."

Palmo answered with a wordless mental bleat of protest.

"Anyhow, even if I supported you, Verret wouldn't, and if you called a council on it, do you think you'd get enough votes to override a divided Headship?"

"So you do support me!"

"No. I see the possibility, but I see what we have to lose. What do we lose by waiting?"

"The Starborn. They'll give up and leave again if they can't find anyone."

"We'd be no worse off."

Palmo had a picture in his head of the skies rolling back and hands reaching out in welcome. It was an ancient image in the religion that, in theory, all the Learned disbelieved, because, also in theory, it bade them wait redemption patiently, a commandment which certainly seemed to forbid re-establishing the old Learning on their own.

Koriam shrugged. "Look, why don't you go get copies of what's been heard and join in trying to break the code—or understand the language," he added, before Palmo objected.

Palmo looked at him with sorrow and some anger. Koriam still saw only possibility where Palmo saw a certainty—or at least, he added honestly, a strong probability. Koriam could not support him. "Thanks, anyway," said Palmo. He pressed his brother's hand and left the cup, hurrying, because his own distress would leave the cup an uneasy place for Koriam, for a while.

Koriam inspected the miniature faces of the red-eel leaves until Palmo started to merge with the rest of the community, then started down the hill. If he couldn't find the flaw in his silicon flake, he could at any rate ask if any news had come in from the agents who sold knowledge to the Brokers of Knowledge, of sound-senders in the lands beyond, or of Thiele.

AMONG THE JUMPERS

Leah's breath was coming in short gasps by the time they reached the top of the rise. The young alien tugged at her impatiently, moving her up the hill more by sheer force of will than by any effort of Leah's. Leah stopped for a moment to rest and looked back at the old woman. When they had left her at the bottom of the hill, Leah had caught a sadness and fear emanating from Jumper-friend, and yet also a sense of determination. She had not understood what it was all about, and Angin had seemed oblivious to the old woman's words. She had already been dragging Leah relentlessly up the hill in her eagerness to start their journey.

With an undignified thump, Leah dropped to the ground. Despite Angin's urgings to get up, Leah found herself not in the slightest inclined to do so. Peace and Mercy! What was she doing starting out on another trip with a third new group of aliens in about as many days? If she ever made it home alive from this one, she'd have enough source material for a lifetime's worth of dissertations.

Angin's noises suggested a total disregard for Leah's scholarly thoughts. Leah also had to admit to herself that her curiosity had been piqued. What were these beings that Angin said had fallen from the sky? And how could a completely other intelligent race exist upon this planet with no one aside from Angin's people discovering them? If the Jumpers had really come from the sky, that meant they were capable of space travel. Could they be the ones sending the radio messages and not Thiele's people?

Leah got up and climbed the final rise with Angin. When she stood atop the ridge, Leah beheld what at first seemed like a field of swaying black trees, decorated in silver and diamonds. Then she realized she looked down on a group of alien beings who towered over the feeble trees clinging to the foot of the hill. Each Jumper must stand well over two meters tall. The Jumpers resembled nothing so much as kangaroos, with large feet, powerful legs, and a huge tail to balance their movement. They gleamed in the sunlight, their black fur patterned in intricate designs of silver. Their dark eyes all turned as one to watch Angin and Leah descend the hill.

Leah had no doubt about their intelligence. The group stood in silence, obviously waiting and knowing for what they waited. As she drew closer, she noticed the creatures were tentacled, all the tentacles covered in soft black fur. Some of the creatures had two tentacles, some four. She wondered if this was a secondary sexual characteristic since she observed no others among them at first glance.

As they walked toward the Jumpers, Leah noticed Angin's face was taking on the same rapt expression it had assumed when she first told Leah about them. Was Angin somehow in communication with them in a way Leah could not share or understand? Leah did feel something coming from the creatures—a silent hum, building in intensity as she approached. She began to feel frightened by it, almost overwhelmed by it. She took several deep breaths and tried to stop hearing the sound that was not really there.

The Jumpers did not appear to move, yet Leah suddenly had the impression all their eyes had focused on her. Slowly, almost imperceptibly, movement began among them, at first like a slight breeze in the trees and then like a gathering wind. The dance became faster, more intricate. Leah quickly lost all awareness of the individual motion of tentacle or head or swaying torso.

The Jumpers became sparkling silver on a field of black. Their dappled coats shone in the sun, becoming waves of brightness against a dark ocean. The dance grew faster yet, until all Leah saw were shimmering lights against a still sky. She stared at the familiar sight of the curving nebula, wondering how the Jumpers could create this vision.

Suddenly, from the frenzied scene before her, two tentacles reached out and wrapped themselves around her. In the second before she was snuggled warmly against a furred back, she saw Angin had been similarly snatched up and nestled securely between a Jumper's back tentacles.

The Jumper who held her began to move. To dance? To run? She had no idea. She only knew the world began to whirl around her at a dizzying rate. She felt the pull of this world recede a little—or thought she did. The sensation was like half-g. She reveled in it. But the visions before her eyes were not nearly so comforting. She closed her eyes tightly and buried her face in the soft, warm fur of the Jumper's back.

How long she remained so, Leah was not sure. After some time, she became aware the Jumper's gait had taken on a smooth, regular pace. She opened her eyes and realized, by the startling change in the landscape around her, that they must now be in the Western Forest—though she could not quite remember when she had heard of the Western Forest before.

Great banks of plumiole grew twice the height of a Jumper, the fronds dark blue, deep purple, rusty red. Green flowers bloomed along the midribs. The plants rustled continuously, appearing to draw back from the Jumpers' passing. The plumiole wavered and shivered; it was not plumiole but a stand of plamon trees they moved among, dark blue trunks rising high. The red-purple winter leaves were shedding as the brighter foliage of summer came out. Scarlet lerioles sang in the branches until the trees changed somehow to Earthly maples, with chickens, Rhode Island Reds that she had known on the space station, improbably perched among the new spring leaves.

Angin opened her eyes to see the lazy meandering of the river at its widest bend. The river stood behind her now, and she was being carried into the forbidden lands of the Western Forest. All around were the forest giants—blackwood, chatolpa, and many hightowers—but sometimes they assumed strange shapes: a blackwood with pale bark of sickly gray; chatolpas whose gray trunks curled up in a spiral to the crowns; hightowers with clusters of velvet black flowers. Slender white trees with leaves of pale blue, unknown in the eastern woods, stood sentinel along the small, dark stream that traveled along to their right, a silent companion. Above the trees, she glimpsed the brilliant blue sky. Over the piled leaf mold of many years lay the drifts of last winter's dark leaves, fallen now to make room for the new spring foliage. Yellow firn was showing fresh growth in the open sunlit glades, with blue-eyes opening their tiny blooms everywhere. Though she saw no other creatures, Angin heard bird calls, some familiar to her but others not: a dreadful cry as of someone in agony, beginning with a high shriek and running down the scale to die away with a moan. Another was less disturbing, but eerie—a call that seemed to come from a great distance, rising at the end to a querying note. It sounded like the words of a language, but the voice was like that of no being she had ever heard. No mindtouch accompanied it.

Angin peered out over the dark fur of the Jumper's tentacle, watching the strange world of the forbidden lands passing her.

Leah surveyed the cityscape with interest. Before her marched a line of skyscrapers not unlike those of Earth but rising from oval or triangular plots of ground. Busy city streets surrounded them, warmed by a yellow sun. Teardrop-shaped vehicles hummed along, occasionally taking to the air to land on platforms set into the buildings. Shop doors were open at the street levels. People spilled out of the open doors and into the small parks at the base of the skyscrapers. A group of musicians played in one of these, a small park bright with red and gold flowers. It was a cheerful, bustling city, one that Earthers could find very appealing, but its inhabitants were not from Earth.

Something tugged at Leah's memory, some reason she should not feel so at home here. Impatiently she pushed it away and let herself float on the thrum of the streetsingers' music, the soft song of windchimes tied in the trees.

Angin turned her head wistfully toward what she hoped was the east. Under the dense growth of the forest, it was hard to tell. She had never been so far out of the sight and sound of her "twin," the Angin River. She found herself wishing for the familiar whispering of the river near her ear, the playful currents teasing her to test her strength against them.

As she found herself growing lonely for home, the Jumpers must have sensed her mood. In that mysterious way that Angin's ears could not hear but her mind perceived, the Jumpers began their Starsong. It started out quietly, like a hum. Then it grew—not louder, but more complicated, like the beachdwellers' dye patterns from far to the South.

Concentrating on the low murmur of the Starsong, Angin closed her eyes and saw a stand of narrow, flexible tubes, their tops widening into open bells. They grew in the shallows of the tree-shadowed Angin river. Striped in yellow and orange like a fossa, the bell reeds ranged in height from knee high to the height of a tall man. As the water pushed at them, they moved, now lifting their bells as if gazing out across the water; now bending their bells toward each other, as if murmuring together in low voices.

Angin realized she was seeing the scene through someone else's eyes but she didn't know whose. This wasn't how the Jumpers pictured this world.

She was floating in the shallow waters, enjoying the warmth of the sun on her round belly. At the same time, she felt the cool waters matting her back hair and washing over her chest occasionally to tease her four nipples, which were already swollen with pregnancy.

(*Pregnancy?* Angin wondered.)

But the whispers and whistles of the winds across the bell reeds were drawing her back to the soft moments of rest in the river. This would be her second set of twins. She was sure they would be twins, though the emanations of the unborn were too feeble and unfocused to tell much, as a general rule. When she had chosen a singlet for a mate, there had been dire predictions that all her children would be born alone, but she had proven them wrong once and would again.

She felt the tug of her twin's mind as she drifted, nearly asleep in the water. Though her twin was almost two days' walk from here, she received her sendings clearly. They had joked about it since Tam had struck out on her own, rather than share her twin's home after her twin took a mate. She had teased Tam that she couldn't run far enough to get her out of her hair.

(*Tam?* Angin wondered. The twin Akashtai lost long before Angin's own birth. Could it be? But who in these woods would give their child that name after the strange end Tam had met in Oshune?)

"You'll drown that way one day," Tam sent, "you and your younglings with you. Get out of the water if you plan to nap, Dorin."

(Dorin? Yes, that had been Akashtai's name in her youth.)

Dorin waded out of the river obligingly. She stretched out in the sun. "Where are you?"

Tam sent images of an inn—strong smells of manure and stale beer and a greasy stew. Tam was off adventuring again and, as usual, trying to be mysterious about what she was up to. Why such games appealed to her sister Dorin had no idea. She wrinkled her nose and sent, "Let's stay here." And they returned to the warm shore of the river. "I don't see why you prefer traipsing around the countryside, staying in places like that, far from your own kin," she added, out of habit.

Tam's answer was a strong surge of feeling, a tantalizing glimpse of the wanderlust that spurred her on, yet Dorin knew there was more to it than that. It wasn't just the traveling that drew her sister, but the people and their intrigues and their power plays and their games. To Dorin, as to most of the village, it all seemed like a bunch of foolishness, but it drew Tam into its wake like the Moon did the Companions. No one knew much about the why of Tam's coming and going with strangers, but nobody approved.

"I want to see the whole world," Tam sent, a plea for her sister's understanding.

"Because you've seen and done everything there is in your own corner of it?" Dorin asked. It was an old argument. She didn't much like the idea of Tam traveling out of range of twintouch, but she knew it would happen one day.

"Don't upset yourself," Tam soothed. "Take your nap, and I'll stay with you for awhile."

Dorin smiled, secretly pleased that her twin was as drawn to the shared Dreaming as she was.

Shared Dreaming, Angin mused. So it must be true that the twintouch for some grew so strong that twins could walk together in sleep into the lands of each other's dreams. No one had ever stopped to tell her what it might feel like to have a twin.

Angin's hand closed on her necklace. A gift from Oshune, her grandmother had always told her. But in her vision of the past, Angin had seen that ring of shells lying against Tam's chest in the dark inn, and Tam had not then gone to Oshune.

"A gift from Oshune," Tam had breezily dismissed the unusual necklace when Dorin asked, and Dorin knew when she was being put off. The circlet of shells, culled from beaches far to the south of Oshune and of such a translucent delicate water pattern that they were certain to be of value this far north, could have come from some lover of Tam's, but Dorin didn't think so. If Tam had been tangled up with somebody who cared enough to obtain such a rare gift for her, Dorin would have known about it, couldn't have avoided knowing about it any more than Tam could have been unaware when the singlet Banon had caught Dorin's eye three harvests back. But, no, Tam didn't seem content with all the regular things everybody wanted from life—good friends, good lovers, good roofs, good harvest—and she was more likely to get excited over why she got the necklace than who gave it to her, over some cursed notion of hers than a flesh and blood person.

But now, two months after Dorin had lost twintouch with Tam, a stranger had brought the necklace and placed it in Dorin's hand and left no message except, "Your sister asked me to bring you this gift from Oshune." The stranger seemed to know nothing more and refused Dorin's offer of hospitality after his long journey. Dorin was left with the necklace and a certain sense that Tam needed her help. She knew instantly that she would leave her second set of twins in the care of her mate's older sister and undertake the road to Oshune.

Angin knew the outcome of that journey. Dorin had gone to Oshune, the place Tam was headed when they had lost twintouch two months earlier, only to discover that Tam had never arrived there. The few people there who seemed to know Tam didn't know her well, and the little they knew about her business they weren't saying. Dorin was frustrated by her inability to get information about her sister, but what concerned her was the lack of twintouch. Traveling all through the streets of Oshune, she had not once detected Tam's presence. Her sister was nowhere within seven days' travel of her—and Dorin began to suspect that Tam had gone even further from her than that, perhaps even to the next world.

Tam had never returned, and what happened to Dorin became a subject of legend among her people, but the truth was never known. Legends said that she had slipped beyond the Veil of Ashven to wrest her sister from the rule of Death. Some said she had succeeded, and Tam lived in the Western forests, beyond the Angin River. Others said she had failed but had bargained with Death for the power to call the Jumpers and to bring Night down upon the world at her command. Still others said she had no power but had only gone mad with the loss of her twin and should have died soon after, as most folks do.

Angin knew the Jumpers were real and that Akashtai had learned to call them. At some point in the past, Akashtai had spent time among the Jumpers and earned her name, which meant Jumper-friend. Angin wished now she had the whole story before her, for she felt it had some bearing on her own journey in the land of the Jumpers.

She rested her head tiredly on the soft back of the Jumper who carried her. She could feel the warmth of the Jumper and smell the wet, raw smell of the soil where the rain had recently drenched the Western Forest. Yet when she closed her eyes, she heard the whisper of the wind in the bell reeds once more. Soon she heard the Starsong joining that whistle and opened her eyes to see a tribe of Jumpers gathered on the western shore of the river. As she, seeing again through the eyes of Dorin, emerged from the reeds and her battle with Death, she knew her first reprieve from the tearing pain that had been a part of her since she lost twintouch with Tam, a pain that had intensified as her journeys had confirmed her suspicions of Tam's death.

The Jumpers stood on the shore—soft, dark creatures with curious pointed faces, their fur sparkling like water droplets in bright sun. It did not surprise Dorin to find these mythical creatures. Nor did it startle her when one of the Jumpers lifted her onto its back and settled her there snugly as a nursing infant. Somehow, she knew they were her reward and her solace for the loss of Tam. The touch of the Jumpers was not twintouch, no, but something comfortable and familiar. She didn't understand their thinking but, as she traveled with them, she could feel how their minds worked together, the whole community in a link that seemed as intimate as twintouch. And while she could not join in that link, it buoyed her spirit.

Coming to her own awareness for a moment, Angin felt a sensation she had never known before and, but for Dorin's memories, might not have recognized. It was unimpeded communion, and yet it had nothing to do with words. It was a little like having someone massage a cramped limb, allowing the blood to flow once more to the aching muscle, warm and relaxing and long awaited. It was Angin's first direct experience of twintouch. Angin opened her eyes in wonder and stared into the eyes of her dark twin.

* * *

A plain of long multicolored grass with snowcapped mountains on the horizon. A wind blowing, and a smell of growing things. No sounds, but an atmosphere of expectancy and life, as if there were wonders to be found, just beyond. Leah raised her head, inhaled deeply, tasting the air. Here was no drag of heavy gravity, straining her muscles, making breathing itself an effort.

She started towards the mountains at an easy lope, the thick turf springing underfoot. The grasses were turquoise and ochre, silver and emerald green. A few times she passed clumps of white flowers nestled in the grass, low to the ground. The scent of this land was herbal rather than flowery. She caught breaths of what might have been clover, mint, or fennel, and between them the smell of living soil. Dew soaked her legs as she ran.

A flight of birds passed, fifty or sixty of them, low enough for her to see their black and scarlet plumage, the breadth of their powerful wings. Their cries were raucous, jovial. Impulsively, she waved as they winged overhead.

She came to the top of a rise and paused a while to look about her. The land sloped down into a shallow valley where a little river ran, noisy and self-assertive. The chatter of water on stone was loud. Silver light bounced off the hurrying waves.

Could she really be here, she wondered suddenly? It had to be real. The Jumpers must have teleportation. What other explanation was possible?

Suddenly conscious of her thirst, she ran down the slope to the river. Kneeling on the bank, she cupped her hands to scoop up the water. It sparkled, flickered like fire, ran out through her fingers, and she was sitting against a tree in the Western Forest, cupping her hands before her, struggling to hold a handful of water that wasn't there.

For an instant she could have sobbed aloud with loss and disappointment. Then fury swallowed every other emotion. Teleportation, hah. Illusion! She was hungry, thirsty, and tired. This world pulled at her—and it was all a cheat.

She glared around the forest clearing. A fire burned in the center, and in a pot over that fire, something was cooking. Presumably, the Jumpers had started the meal for them, though none of those strange creatures now remained near the fire. Leah saw shimmering lights moving among the trees and guessed it was the Jumpers engaging in their nighttime rituals. Leah revised her estimate of the Jumpers. Not *hostile*, no, but still dangerous.

Angin was seated on the ground nearby. Leah felt her frustration turn to anger. There was her native guide, seeming more out of it than Leah herself. Leah pulled herself to her feet, walked over, and sat down beside Angin. She shook the girl's shoulders, trying to rouse her. Angin's head lolled back and, for the first time since they entered the Western Forest, Leah got a good look at Angin's face. Alien or not, there was no mistaking the expression on the girl's face: Angin's eyes were open and unseeing, gazing into total joy, into glory.

THIELE'S RIDE

Beast trotted down the well-worn gravel path to Ryl's house. Thiele had had a weary two days' ride since leaving Leah with Akashtai. First there was the journey back eastward, a night's sleep, and then north. She'd spent the second evening camped within sight of the road; it was now mid-morning. Thiele initially planned to go directly home, but as she thought about Leah, she became more and more anxious. What if, as Leah had suggested, something happened to her on the way home? She was the only Philosopher who knew about Leah; if she became ill or injured or captured, the knowledge would end with her. She could not risk it. She had to go to Ryl's to try to get word back home.

Fortunately, the road home and the road to Ryl's house were the same for a long way northward. She passed only a few travelers; none gave her more than a passing glance. All she had to do when she changed her mind was turn eastward when she saw the house through the forest.

Thiele tethered Beast to the post at the bottom of the steps. Beast whickered; Thiele patted his nose and scratched his neck. After giving him a cursory examination to see he was well, she turned to the house. It was built of darkleaf wood, a large two-story wooden structure with a porch. Stairs led down to the paved landing where Thiele now stood. Hearing the creak of hinges, she looked up. Ryl had stepped onto the porch deck, wiping his hands on an apron.

"Thiele! Well met! I had a mind for company today; the wife and sons left for her twin's wedding yesterday, so I'm all alone here. I thought I'd do the spring baking while I had the kitchen to myself. Won't you come in?"

The odor of fresh-baked pastries made Thiele's mouth water. She nodded.

When they were seated at the kitchen table, each with a mug of hot spiced cider and a fresh, warm tart, Thiele said, "I need to use your sound-sender to call home. I...." She stopped when she saw Ryl's stricken expression. "What's wrong?"

"There was a transmission. It wasn't from the other houses or your home, Thiele. It was like nothing I ever heard before. It seemed like gibberish to me. But someone else was signaling; that was a fact. We got the order to shut down pending further instructions. It's been quiet ever since. I can't send anything for you. If the Crowns or—heavens forbid!—the Veen have invented sound-senders, I can't give away this location."

Thiele chewed thoughtfully, considering what he said. She swallowed. "No...no, it can't be them. I was just at the Mullen Ruins in Veen territory and talking to a Crowns captain. It has to be Leah's people."

"Who?"

She leaned forward, excited. "I found a being from another world. Her vessel crashed near the ruins. An imperial troop brought her under guard to the inn where I was staying. I found her and took her to a friend of mine, west of here. She's there now. I have to tell them this at home."

"A being from another world?" He was skeptical.

"If you had seen her, you would know." She visualized Leah for him.

He sat back in the chair, startled. "By the stars, it is...."

"You see now why I have to get a message out."

"I see why I can't let you send one. If the Veen have sound-senders, or the—"

"But it *isn't* them. It's Leah's people, the ones that are on the yellow moon, right now."

"No."

She had a fleeting thought of waiting until Ryl was distracted and sneaking into the attic to use the sound-sender herself.

"No, you don't," he said firmly.

She sighed. The trouble with talking to friends was that sometimes one's guard slipped.

"However," he said, "I'll pass on your message to the next house down the road. Kron is out gathering wood, but he should be here by midday. I can send him."

"I can get the message out faster by riding home myself," grumbled Thiele.

"I'm sorry, but that's how it has to be," he said.

She put her guard up as she took another bite of pastry. That would make him suspicious, she knew, but she wanted some privacy to think. Briefly, she considered knocking him out and working the sound-sender herself, but that was a rotten thing to do to an old friend and might not work anyhow. Besides, if they weren't using the sound-senders, there might not be anyone on the other end to receive the message.

He waited patiently for her to speak again. She could sense he was not offended by her retreating into her own thoughts. In fact, it seemed as if he could sense what conclusion she had just made.

"Very well," she said. "But if a message sent through the chain of houses won't reach home much faster than I will, I may as well go get Leah and bring her home myself." She sighed as it occurred to her that this would mean she would miss her chance to conceive this season. There would be other seasons, of course, but what about Palmo? Would he wait or turn to someone else? Perhaps he would understand. One thing she was sure of, and that was a being from another world was a one-time opportunity she could not walk away from. More than that, Leah was a friend now; even if she were not from another world, Thiele could not leave her, in honor, to the dubious fate the Veen offered her.

Ryl was speaking. "If that's what you want, I'll send Kron out this afternoon. I'll pack some supplies for you before you go."

"Thank you." Thiele remembered her packs. "As long as I'm sending things by you anyway, I have some valuable electronic parts with me. Will you see they get home, too?"

"Gladly."

"One more thing. If by chance Leah and I do not meet on the road, I have told her to come here. If she arrives without me, send her on her way if you can, or wait for me to join her, whichever you think best."

"I'll help her as I can."

By midday, Thiele was packed and ready to go again. Kron had returned. He groomed Beast before washing up for dinner. After the meal, Thiele rode southwest; Kron rode his own mount, an ambler, northeast.

Finding Leah again, Thiele knew, was a more complicated matter than simply retracing her route. She had to guess which path Akashtai might set Leah on and try to keep to that general direction. Once she had given mental instructions to Beast, she let him pick the way so she could keep her mind open to contact. Perhaps when she got close enough to Leah, she would be able to pick up her location telepathically.

In midafternoon, Thiele got a disturbing impression of a large group coming northward along the road in her direction. Quickly, she guided Beast into the woods. They hid in a glade. She closed her mind so they could not sense her presence. Unfortunately, that meant she couldn't pick up their thoughts, either, to identify them. As they passed, she peered through the brush as best she could but saw nothing but the movement of riders, and a splash of color which might be an imperial emblem on a shield or flag.

After allowing time for them to get out of range, Thiele slowly opened her thoughts again. She picked up nothing discernible. With a sigh of relief, she mounted Beast again to resume her search.

By sunset, Thiele had become discouraged. She hoped she had not come across Leah because Leah had not left Akashtai's. If they had crossed paths, it might be days before they would meet again. Patting Beast's neck, she said, "Time to look for a place to sleep, I think."

As she was turning Beast aside, a flicker of a thought caught her attention. Leah? She increased her sensitivity. Yes, Leah. It had to be. Southwards, on or near the road. She urged Beast to a canter. Yes, around the next bend. Confidently, she turned the corner, then reined in abruptly. She had nearly collided with Matvar.

THE JOURNEY HOME

Leah started her morning damp and cold. The small cooking fire had burned out in the night, and no one had come to tend it. With a groan, Leah pulled herself up from the ground and shuffled through the motions of getting ready for the day. Angin remained where she was the night before, her expression unchanged.

Just as Leah began to wonder what had become of the Jumpers, they started to emerge from the nearby forest. She blinked fiercely, trying to focus her eyes on them in to study them objectively. When she looked at them, she again had the sensation that they moved, that their appearance shifted before her eyes. The harder she tried to see them, the more disorienting the illusion became. Finally, she gave up.

The Jumpers moved in closer to her, and she saw them as a quick blur of silver-patterned darkness. Soft tentacles lifted her, and she closed her eyes.

When she opened them again she looked out of the Jumper's eyes onto a dying world. She was standing on a surface like gritty concrete. The air was harsh, choking. The buildings were blocky, like fortresses. She could not make out the colors of the walls, and the tops were hidden in an ugly haze. The life emanations of the people inside were muted, dimly visible through the darkness of the air.

She drew in a breath of air that felt thick and tainted. This person through whom Leah saw the Jumpers' home world had lived through the start of many lives and also remembered lives before her own. This person recalled the younger days of the planet when the air was bright and the lights of the people shone clearly.

This person carried a smaller one on her back, as the Jumpers had carried Leah and Angin, with her back tentacles. A child, Leah realized. Thus far among the Jumpers of Autumn World Leah had seen no children.

She saw this child now through the Jumper's eyes. It was an ever-changing pattern of color, a constant dance of motion, a little being who had not yet learned to conform its emanations to its physical structure. It was the joy of its people.

Yet the adult Jumper was at the spaceport to take the child away from its home planet, to give the child a future on a new world.

Leah realized the new world must be Autumn World. So the spaceports on Autumn World had been built by peoples from other worlds. And, with that thought, she suddenly saw the new world to which the Jumpers had come.

The Jumpers delighted in this planet teeming with life, from the faint warm light of the bacteria in the rich soil to the colorful herds of bosorn and lopers on the plains. Most of all they loved the forests: the gentle glow of sap rising in the trees, the fragile tendrils of new life reaching out from the earth everywhere, the fertile bright plants that gave them their food.

Eventually the ships no longer returned, yet the Jumpers remained. They held themselves aloof from the young cultures native to their new world, leaving them to grow in their own ways, and withdrew into the Western Forest—close enough to the Forbidden Lands to insure their privacy, far enough from them to keep their people safe.

The Jumpers did not build on their new world. They had seen, first on their home planet and now in the star culture of Autumn World, the ravages of technology upon a planet. They lived simply in the forest, gathering food from its natural abundance, building nothing and tending nothing and forming nothing save the close mind-link of their community.

Years of life layered themselves over the Jumpers' history, and a new sadness came to their people: few children were born here and, of those born, not many lived. For all of their joy in this world, it could not seem a true home with no future, no children. The Jumpers lived long lives, and yet there began to be deaths among them. They yearned toward the young lives around them, the short-lived natives who never seemed to grow beyond childhood before their lives ended.

The sociologist in Leah wondered why their race could no longer keep up a sufficient replacement rate. Among Earthers, women often experienced amenorrhea when they first shifted from one planet to another or from station to planetside. Sometimes, when altitude or gravity changes were too great, the difficulty was prolonged, and special medical treatment was needed to restore the balance. Could the Jumpers have experienced a similar, permanent disruption of their breeding cycle?

The Jumpers might not appreciate her people's use of technology, but she suspected they might warm to it if they ever saw the children of her home station.

She was floating with a group of children, with their teachers, in the stationary ring; they were lined up, all politely holding on to grab the rail so as not to drift in each other's way. Outside the long, curved window spread all of space. Moon to the left, Earth turning slowly off to the right. A shuttle was approaching below. They watched as a crew in power suits moved out, attached tow cables, and rode the outside of the shuttle as it was slowly drawn in under the curve of the habitat. Teachers pointed out the lights of other stations, a second shuttle heading away, and most importantly, a Hultzu ship. Sunlight glittered on the polished hull as it moved toward the contact wheel.

She was older. With other senior students, all kitted up properly in their own power suits, she moved carefully over a decrepit inter-station scooter. Under the watchful eye of a couple of master engineers, they worked on repairs. She might be majoring in sociology, but all the kibbutz children had to learn basic engineering and maintenance...now she was inside looking out again. The contact wheel was dwindling in the distance. She was conscious of a person beside her, five bodies—a Querlitzen watching with her. She was on a Jheehan ship leaving the solar system.

She was standing in the farm on the station, looking across the center column to the haze of green on the other side. It was "day" on the station; the panels had been opened to admit sunlight from the reflectors. Around her was the network of nutrient pipes and misting booms. The tanks were lush with the green of tomatoes and cabbage, cucumber vines, carrot and potato tops.

The warm, humid air carried a faint scent of ripening melons. Soon they would be harvesting the current crop, then the tanks would be stripped and cleaned, a new planting begun. It was good to be home.

Steam rolled out of the machine as Leah opened the heavy door in the machine's side and slid out another hot tray of dishes. While most people were content with plastic pouches and containers during the week, everyone enjoyed the use of traditional ware on Shabbat. Leah liked the colorful dishes, their hardness, the heavy weight of them as she hoisted them from the tray, still warm, and slung them onto their respective stacks. She liked the clatter as she did that. It gave her a sense of authority and purposefulness she never got from dropping plastic into the recycler.

Each afternoon before Shabbat, she volunteered in the station kitchen, enjoying the hard physical labor of manually preparing food for the whole station, of the cleaning and cooking and decorating that went into the station's weekly festival. Leah enjoyed handling the special dishes they used for this day. They had come from Earth, and she had always thought of them as bits of glazed Earth themselves. There was something in their hand-painted faces, their uniqueness, their very permanence—these trays wouldn't be recycled; it was these same dishes she would use again next week, and not some reconstituted version of them—that gave her a sense of the Earth that made them.

She was flying alone, in the up-axis recreation area, soaring in weightlessness. It was very quiet. She moved with effortless skill, circling and diving, controlling her flight with easy flicks of an ankle or wrist. A bird must feel like this in the skies of Earth; but a bird must come down, and she thought she could fly forever. Time had stopped, and there was nothing more to life than flying.... A sense of urgency grew in her mind, breaking the spell. Something she should be doing, a job she must finish. What was it?

This isn't true, she realized suddenly. It's another illusion.

The station faded around her, and heaviness returned to her limbs. She was leaning against the ridged, ivory bark of a pomponia. Angin stood behind her, and the crowd of Jumpers encircled them. The Jumpers seemed still for once, and Leah took advantage of this to try to examine the tall beings, to count them. There were fifteen in the group, with curious sharp faces, their eyes large. Suddenly it seemed wrong to Leah that she should be able to see them clearly.

She realized it must be because every one of them had focused its attention on Angin. All eyes were turned to the girl, and Leah felt again the build of the silent hum that had terrified her at the start of their journey. She remembered the sharp longing she had sensed in the Jumpers, and she immediately feared for Angin.

Angin's face took on a new aliveness, and she seemed, for the first time since they had entered the Western Forest, to actually see the Jumpers rather than look beyond them. Leah didn't know what was happening, but she didn't like it. She grabbed Angin's shoulders and shook them. Angin brushed her hands away easily, but otherwise did not break her communion with the Jumpers.

Desperate, Leah took Angin's face between her hands and tried to force Angin's attention, to make eye contact. She called Angin's name repeatedly. Still no response.

Then she tried thinking at Angin. If telepathy held her, maybe telepathy could reach her. She touched Angin's face again, sending images of her need for Angin, the importance of her mission, how lost she would be without Angin's guidance.

Angin blinked.

Leah thought of Jumper-friend and her fears of losing her grandchild to the Jumpers. *She needs you,* she thought. *I need you. You don't belong there. Come back!*

Suddenly Angin *was* back. Her eyes widened in disbelief. Then she crumpled to the ground, wailing her grief. Disconcerted, Leah knelt beside Angin and smoothed the hair on her back. She made comforting noises and tried to send soothing thoughts to the girl. It was a long time before Angin moved.

When Angin sat up, she was composed, her face telling Leah little about what she felt. Leah sensed the girl's sadness but was at a loss as to what to do. Angin stood slowly and began to walk toward the east. Leah followed her.

These woods were more open than the heavy forests farther south. The trees were more widely spaced, the varieties different. On the open ground, winter-bleached firn grew almost knee-high, with the yellow blades of spring starting up from below. On rockier stretches where the firn was sparse, there were broad patches of tiny flowers. The petals varied in color, but each one had a startling deep blue center. Other flowers produced green heads that reminded Leah of cotton balls. Clumps of tall, gray, leafless stems rattled in the wind. The most common tree vaguely resembled an Earthly evergreen. The branches were covered with clusters of thick fleshy "needles," mostly dark bronze in color. These had a strong resinous smell. The new spring clusters were bright orange; when she touched one in passing, her fingers came away covered with stickiness. She wiped them on her coverall, wishing for a bath and a change of clothes. There were bird songs everywhere—a regular peep-peep, a gurgling whistle, a plaintive fluting, sharp cries, and tapping sounds.

When they came to the curve of the stream, they found it fully occupied by large green, white-breasted birds, diving and splashing in the water.

Angin ran forward with a shout, waving her arms wildly, and the whole flock took off, wings thrumming. "Get out, you stupid birds!"

She considered a moment, then started upstream. Leah followed. They came to a spot where water bubbled from a spring and here, after some careful inspection, Angin pronounced the water drinkable. Angin knelt and drank easily from her own cupped hands; Leah imitated her as best she could, thankful her coverall was water repellent. They sat down and shared a sketchy meal from Angin's pack. Leah felt pretty safe now with the blue kerm and nibbled on some of the fruit. Afterward she fell asleep.

She came to with Angin shaking her and immediately sensed the girl's concern.

"We must go on now—are you all right?"

Leah sat up. She *was* tired. She leaned forward, head on knees, breathing deeply. It might not be far, but it was a long way for someone not used to this gravity.

"Are you all right? Can you keep going?"

"I think so." She thought about her injured arm. She hadn't even been aware of it during the trip with the Jumpers, and certainly there had been no pain these last few hours...she undid the bandage. It was draggled and soiled now, but underneath the wound was clean and looked nearly healed. She decided it would be safe to leave it uncovered. She got to her feet, bracing herself against a nearby tree trunk. Some cautious stretching and bending loosened her muscles, restored some tone.

Overhead, great islands of cloud were sailing past. The air was colder. "I'm all right," she told Angin. "We can go on now."

They went back downstream. The birds had returned, raucous and lively. Angin scared them away again, and the two of them crossed the water where a series of rocky ledges formed natural stepping stones. They went slowly, Angin helping Leah most of the way, then off through the woods once more.

By now Leah was too tired to notice much, fully occupied with the need to keep putting one foot ahead of the other. Angin had to slow her own pace. They came to a low ridge, and Leah had to climb it in stages, pausing to catch her breath and rest several times before they reached the top and came to level ground. Angin virtually hauled her up the last slope. Now Angin walked beside Leah, keeping a close watch on her.

She guided Leah carefully around tangled mats of thorn, warning of their poisonous qualities; pointed out a tumble of stone where tiny furry animals dashed in and out of burrows; and speculated on the meal they might expect to be given when they arrived at their destination.

A meal sounded good to Leah, too. She felt starved and wondered again if they had eaten anything during the time with the Jumpers. Surely they had, or she would be even weaker now, but it was definitely time for another meal. If nothing else, she could stuff herself with bread, and some of those vegetables seemed to be pretty safe as well.

They came out of the trees, and Angin pointed ahead. There was the road again, the old road of the ancients, cutting straight through the shallow, wooded hills. Leah felt a surprising burst of energy now that the end of the trip was near. She followed Angin with more alacrity than she had been able to manage all afternoon.

They walked north for some distance, then turned off to the east on a rutted gravel road. A large house was visible through the trees.

Leah looked about eagerly. The house was two stories, built of smoothly finished, squared-off logs. A wide porch fronted the entire building, with steps leading down to a landing paved with flagstones. It looked solid and prosperous. There were other equally substantial buildings, barns and sheds, grouped around an irregularly shaped courtyard. A fence of stripped, woven branches surrounded a paddock where several animals grazed—ornits like the one Thiele rode, and little pony-sized creatures with long hair and small horns behind their ears. Some of these came to poke their noses over the fence at the newcomers, making noises that sounded absurdly like a cat's meow. A big maroon and gray striped fossa stood up near the largest barn and chattered at them. Leah watched it nervously, having read of attack dogs used on Earth in the old days, but it stayed where it was, apparently content with announcing their presence. Above them the door opened, and a man poked his head out, glancing once at the fossa, then at the two standing below. His expression cleared. He stepped out, holding the door open, beckoning them in.

"Thiele told me to look for you!" he announced. "Come inside, be welcome."

He opened the door wide, then came down to help Leah up the steps, looking at her with friendly curiosity. He knows who—and what—I am, she thought.

She was disappointed Thiele was not there. But Ryl was certain Thiele could take care of herself, and would learn of Leah's arrival. She was not sure if he meant a telepathic message could carry so far or if he meant to send people to find Thiele or leave word for her, but she assumed he knew what he was talking about.

She sighed with contentment as she settled into Ryl's kitchen. No hut or cave or cold ground here, but a clean, warm house.

Leftovers from Ryl's own lunch were still cooling on the stove. He invited her to choose food that appealed to her. She delicately sniffed at and tasted the offerings, finally choosing setony and a porridge made from kerm. These appeared to be the staple foods, at least in this area, for which she was grateful. Angin accepted these plus a mixture of other vegetables in a thick sauce and a large pastry. It looked good. Leah decided she would try a little, after the rest of her meal. It must be mostly kerm, after all.

While Ryl busied himself with the food, Angin sipped a cup of something milky. Leah decided to wait for what Ryl called sourstrap tea to get hot—it smelled good. Angin was quiet, her mind closed. Was she thinking of the Jumpers? Leah was worried.

On the station, Leah would fly to think her worries out, but she could not do that here. Instead, she wandered about the house slowly, into the wide front parlor and back again, examining the contents, her curiosity taking charge of her. The furnishings were made of fine, black wood with simple, clean patterns beautifully carved. The padded chairs were covered with a heavy, bright-colored cloth. They had a faint, not unpleasant odor of rhizo, and she thought the plant must be used, dried, for the stuffing. The ceilings were high and the walls mostly bare except in the kitchen, where utensils and tools and shelves had been attached to them. Ryl was a man of substance, she decided, although he did not stand on ceremony as a person of similar status might in an equivalent culture on historic Earth.

Along the base of one wall of the kitchen, something gleamed. Leah turned to look at it and saw a gap where a plank of wood was out of place. Inside was a broken cord, the insulation stripped back at each end, showing the bare copper wire.

Ryl pursed his lips. "Put it back, will you?" he said, jutting an elbow at the plank, as his hands were full. "I'll splice it later. "

Leah stared at the wire, dumbfounded, for a moment, before she lifted up the plank and shoved it back into its place. Peace and Mercy, she thought, I may have done it upside down and backwards, but I've done it: I've completed my mission and found the people who sent the radio signal.

VALAD'S RIDE

Valad was in a grand mood. His spies had brought him word that Matvar had been seen riding north on the imperial road. Better yet, Thiele had been spotted there, too, about a day's ride ahead of Matvar. Within reach, now, was his beloved; whether he found her first or Matvar found her and delivered her to him did not matter. She should be his within a day or so.

As Valad trotted north, retainers in tow, his lovely-footed Thiele was foremost on his mind. Ah, the sport she gave him, pretending to run from his guards yet going quietly with them whenever they caught her. A truly worthy mate she would be, yes, and as much in love with him as he was with her. Why else would her heartbeat and breathing quicken when she was with him? Why else would she listen so intently while he explained the virtues of the Veen philosophies? Most of all, why else would she come to his province so often, that backwoods dump where his fungus-footed, hammer-toed, no-good twin brother Rolad plotted to have him sent? ...And they called those with identical twins "Blessed," Valad thought to himself. Rolad was surely no blessing to him.

The two of them, youngest of four sets of twins, got little enough parental attention, and when they did, Mother always seemed to prefer Rolad, holding him in her lap while he, Valad, played at her feet. What exquisite feet Mother had. Mother always went barefoot in the house.

Perhaps Thiele, too, would stop wearing shoes in the house once they were mated. Ah, Thiele: how cleverly she had escaped, the night he had proposed. The guards hadn't even seen her go, swore they hadn't, even when Valad had them beaten for their inattentiveness. Of course, he could not treat Thiele so, even though he suspected the guards' lapse was her doing, really not the guards' fault. Still, he would have to do something to her to assert his authority when he caught her. Something delicate, but forceful. Now that was a challenge. His father walked with a limp because of what his mother had done to him on their wedding night. Mother always said that Father abducting her from her own father was one thing—she was more than willing to marry a hot-blooded rogue like Father—but locking her in a room while Father went out celebrating with his friends had gone beyond the bounds of good taste. Women were touchy about such things.

In the end, though, Valad was certain that his will would prevail. He would allow Thiele a study and a few books and papers to keep her happy, and she would settle down soon enough to be a good Veen mother. And, ah, the life of a family man! Lying by the fire with the feet of his beloved on his chest while the brats tore up the furniture around them. Twin boys, to raise a father's ire, or twin girls, whose suitors he could bully. Such quaint tiny little feet children had. What times he would have, dumping them into their beds, watching them cower under the covers at his approach. Who could ask for more?

Ahead on the road, a peasant man stood, pointing eastward into the forest. Valad reined in the kurval to look. Through the trees stood a large wooden house. A gravel road led to it. A jumble of thought impressions came from there. No doubt that was where his beloved was. He directed his chief retainer, Frond, to toss a few coins to the peasant. The man scraped for the coins, bowed, and scurried away.

"Surround the house," Valad said to Frond. "Do it quietly, lest she be warned and try to escape. Do not harm her."

The retainers spread out.

Valad rode to the house, a smile on his face. Within moments, she would be his, and then…ah, what a wonderful life they would—

A fossa stood up and began chattering its alarm at the presence of strangers.

"Shut up!" said Valad and raced up the stairs, then fell flat on the porch as his spiked boot heel caught in a flaw in the wood. Swearing, he pulled his foot loose and got to his feet. He glared at Frond, but Frond stood quietly behind him. Not even a smirk could be seen on his retainer's face. Good. Valad turned and knocked on the door.

A man answered, and the fossa gave up its futile complaint. At the sight of the imperial badge the man said, humbly, "Yes, Magistrate?"

Valad drew himself up to his full height. "I've come for Thiele. Tell her that her beloved has come to claim her."

The man looked startled. Then he said, "There is no one by that name here, Magistrate."

"Nonsense. She was seen riding to this house."

"She is not here, Magistrate," the man insisted. "On my honor."

Valad snorted. He turned to Frond and the other two retainers behind him. "She is playing games again. Hiding." He pushed the man aside. "We will find her," he said as he strode into the house.

Before the man could protest, Valad walked through the house into the kitchen in back. The man followed.

"Where is she?" demanded Valad. He heard Frond and the other two walking in behind him. The man of the house glanced to the ceiling, then turned away quickly, as if he'd betrayed a secret.

Valad cast his eyes and thoughts in that direction. "There's no one there," he said, annoyed. "You cannot distract me so easily. Where is she?"

"As I said, Magistrate, she is not here."

Frond motioned to the other retainers. They moved toward the man, threateningly. The intended victim cringed but didn't move.

Valad sighed. "No use to question him," he said, calling his men off. "She has probably influenced him to say nothing. Come, let's look around. I sense other thoughts here."

Retracing his steps to the middle of the house, Valad spotted a door. Testing the handle, he found it was locked. He smiled. "Ah, hiding from me, are you?" He turned. "Open the door," he said to the house man. When he hesitated, Valad added, "Or we break it."

He produced a key and opened the door.

When Valad pushed, a young woman rushed out. She tripped a guard, sending him sprawling. Frond blew the whistle to signal those outside to come in. The woman hit the other guard in the lungs. He doubled over. While she was thus occupied, Frond grabbed her from behind and held fast. Before she could struggle free, another guard came in from outside. Between them, they held her still.

Valad frowned at her. "That's not Thiele! Hold her anyway. She may be able to tell us something."

Hearing noises from inside the room, Valad peered around the door. A figure crept to an open window. When Valad shouted a warning, it started, tripped on the rug, and landed flat, stomach down. Valad strode into the room. The figure thrashed like a beached water-breather. Valad walked to it and turned it over with his boot. He grimaced. It was one of those feeble-minded freak births, and somehow it had grown to maturity. Then, with a shock, he matched the shape before him with the image he had read in Matvar's mind, an image that Matvar had somehow linked with Thiele. While it struggled feebly to get up, Valad smiled. So…again his beloved was sporting with him, leaving this thing in her place and planting a clue in Matvar's mind to lead him to her. Very well. He, Valad, could play games, too.

Reaching down, he took it by the hand and pulled…her…to her feet. Then he pushed her down on a nearby couch. Hovering over her as she sat, he carefully reached to her thoughts. Thiele? Yes, the thing recognized her image. Name of thing?

The thing answered, "Lay-ahh."

Valad straightened up and turned to his men, who were visible through the open doorway. Pointing to Leah, he said, "This one will come with us."

Frond indicated his prisoner. "What about this one?"

Valad looked around. The door with the key still in its hole caught his eye. He pointed. "Put her in there. Take the key."

Frond obeyed. The woman struggled fiercely, but Frond and the other guard managed to throw her in and shut the door. She pounded on the door as the lock clicked.

Valad reached down to pull Leah up again, but his eyes wandered to her feet. Overwhelmed by curiosity, he drew his arm back and knelt instead. He extended Leah's leg as far as it would go so she could not kick him. Carefully, he removed her footwear and stocking. He looked, turned away, and looked again. Grotesque. A skinny little foot with an extra toe at the end. The small flat claws on top of each toe were a bright red, shot through with white or blue or green. Whether they were naturally that way or painted, Valad didn't care. He didn't want to see appendages like that again. Clumsily, he replaced the stocking and shoe. Matvar must be a pervert to want such a woman.

ANGIN'S RESCUE

Angin learned—by trying the knob, throwing herself at the door, and peering into the keyhole—the door was locked. She had never seen a lock before in her life and now, in one afternoon, she had twice been put behind a door with a lock.

The first time she had had the lock explained briefly before she was hastily shoved behind it. She was told it would stand as an obstacle between herself and beings who might harm Leah. This time, however, she had no illusion that these rough men used the lock for anyone's protection. Clearly they had made the device serve them by depriving her of a free range of motion. What right had they? Angin was outraged.

The room she was in was small and dim and full of baking smells, cooking utensils, and shelves of jarred grains and flours. Racks of freshly-baked breads and pastries sat on the top shelves. Angin clearly wouldn't starve even if she were in the room for a long time, which she had no intention of being. She intended to get *out*. Now.

There was no window in the room and only one door. A narrow door with a lock wedging one side into the door frame. She peered at the other side of the door to see what held that side in place. Two hinges, like any door in her own village. Even if she knew nothing about locks, she understood hinges. She located a large knife and got to work knocking the pins loose.

One pin sat loose in the hinge at the top of the door. She had little more to do than give it one quick tap and slide it out. The bottom pin was more stubborn, held in its groove not only by tension but by the accumulation of dirt and dust that blew about closer to the floor. She had given it its final tug when she heard a familiar voice on the other side of the door.

"Angin, they took the key with them, and I haven't been able to find its double," Ryl's voice called. "But don't worry. We'll get you out of there."

Angin was not particularly worried, but before she could say so, Ryl called out, "I'm going to try something. Stand clear of the door."

Angin, thinking it better not to argue with such a request, hurried to the rear of the pantry. There was a large thud as Ryl's body met with the door, a shattering sound as the door jamb splintered at the lock. The door heaved inward, fell to the floor, and Ryl skidded in a heap to Angin's feet. Angin stared at him, unimpressed.

"Well," Ryl said, dusting himself off busily, "I guess we've gotten you out now."

"Thank you," Angin said and marched out of the small room. "Where would they have taken her?"

Ryl shrugged. "Perhaps to Valad's home. Or perhaps they followed Thiele back to your village. It's hard to say."

"Well, I have to follow them. I promised my grandmother I would deliver her safely."

"And you have," Ryl said soothingly. "I don't see what else you can do. You can't take on a Magistrate by yourself. Since Valad is following Thiele, Thiele will find Leah and rescue her when Valad catches up with her. I think your best bet, my young friend, would be to return to your people."

"She's my responsibility." Ryl had no way of knowing how painful the decision to fulfill that obligation had been for her, and perhaps he was only now beginning to realize her determination.

Ryl sighed. "You could decide to take on the world by yourself," he began, and Angin bristled. "Or you could twin with me in my efforts to do something useful."

That hit home. Angin maintained her stubborn pose, but listened more attentively. "How?"

"There are two other Learned Ones in this area. They will be of more help to Thiele and your friend than you could be. If you set out on the North Road immediately, you can catch up to my hired man, Kron. He started out after midday on an ambler. If I lend you an ornit, you'll catch up to him before nightfall."

"Why should I?"

"Because you traveled with that Leah. You can tell the Learned Ones about her. She really is from the stars?"

Angin smiled. After her recent adventures, *that* part had come to seem a very small thing. "Yes."

"Yes, I suppose she is." He blinked and shook himself.

Angin's mind was still on his earlier statement: she could tell the Learned Ones about Leah. "You mean, go all the way north to the home of the Learned Ones? You want me to go? Me?"

"No, your twin," Ryl said sarcastically.

Angin was momentarily startled, wondering how he knew, how anyone could have known about her twin—but of course he didn't. The unaccustomed feel of intimacy still clung to her like the scent of golden lace did to her river-washed hair. As Angin sat here in Ryl's warm kitchen, her twin seemed as tangible to her as the river flowers. Angin still did not know how the Jumpers had reached into her deepest desires to create her dark twin, the faceless presence that communicated to her without language and yet understood Angin more thoroughly than anyone else ever had. How could *that* have been an illusion?

Yet it was an illusion. Angin remembered the sense of waking when Leah's voice began to reach her. Long before she had been able to tear herself away enough to answer Leah, she had heard Leah's words. The words were telling Angin she was needed, as no one had ever seemed to need her before. Leah was demanding she fulfill her promise, accept her responsibility, and Angin had realized that she must. Her fight back to consciousness was the hardest thing she had ever done. It was harder than the nightmares where you knew you had to wake up, had to wake up if you were to survive, and yet your limbs had turned to stone and your body seemed so far away and unresponsive that you could not even will one eyelid to rise. It was harder than sitting at her family's dinner table on holidays, watching all the twins giggle and share thoughts and kick each other under the table, while she knew the whole time that she was the only one in her family who was truly alone. It was harder than the time she'd lost her footing in the south caves and had to pull herself free from the rocks and then walk the long road home, the air hot even down by the river and her broken arm jolting every step of the way. Deciding to wake up and leave the Western Forest with Leah had been harder than all of those things put together. Even though she realized her twin was not one single being but an illusion the Jumpers created together, Angin had not been able to imagine leaving the sense of twintouch for her own solitary life. Yet, somehow, she had done it. The pain of separation was still fresh in her, but she was, after all, finding her return to solitary life—well, not entirely solitary.

"Well," Ryl finally demanded, his patience exhausted. "What do you say? Should I get my ornit ready?"

"And me riding all the way to the north lands?" Angin grinned. "Better make it a kurval."

CAPTURE

The stream was so close they had been able to hear it from the road. They had gone only to fill their water bottles. It should have taken no time at all. Yet they had been lost in the forest for two days. Matvar was certain it was two days; Haspar and Raspid swore it was three. At night, they had tried to camp, but their fires would not stay lit. Voices had mocked them from the dark forest, and they had had terrible dreams. Matvar had heard his dead brother calling to him.

Late in the afternoon, they stumbled onto the road once again, within sight of the place where they had left it. The soldiers were greatly cheered, but Matvar was close to despair. He had lost his fragile twintouch with the Starborn woman. He did not even remember when it had gone.

He knew it was time to give up the search, to return to the inn and relieve Arunesh. He had duties to perform. A report must be made, even without living evidence of the Return. There was the body of the dead creature. All was not lost. He tried to console himself with these thoughts, but sometime in the last two days his visions of glory in the city had become less important than the empty place in him—Rudvar's place—that had been filled again just long enough to remind him of what it was like to be whole. Her ugliness and the strangeness of her mind no longer mattered. But she was gone.

It was too late to ride far before dark. Without much hope, Matvar decided to try going north while there was light enough and gave orders accordingly. He might pick up a trace again. Someone might have seen her. Even now someone approached. They felt a single mind and heard a faint scuffling in the dust. A woman riding an ornit came full speed around the bend and pulled to a stop, narrowly avoiding a collision with the five kurvals. She was very surprised.

Matvar glared at the Learned One. He had wanted to find her only slightly less than he wanted to find the Sky Dweller, but the sight of her, alone, annoyed him inexpressibly. He had become convinced—he had not yet thought to ask himself why—that where one was, the other would be. She had no right to untwin his search.

Thiele made a business of relaxing on her saddle and bowed to him. "Greetings of the evening, your Honor," she said. Her emanations were innocent: here I am, going about my not-at-all-interesting business, which is unworthy of your attention. I am very respectful toward you, in spite of being one of those harmless wandering eccentrics. Altogether insignificant, that's what I am. You have more important things to do than bother with me.

It was enough for the four soldiers, but it did not deceive Matvar even briefly. She had been not quite fast enough to conceal the blast of surprise she had felt on seeing him instead of Leah. He knew she had expected to find someone else. The Sky Dweller?

"Evening's greeting, Learned One," Matvar replied gruffly. He forced restraint upon himself in spite of the turbulence and weariness within him. "This is a fortunate meeting. I have been wishing to speak with you."

"I am at your service, your Honor." Thiele's initial shock and consciousness of disaster were receding as she began to understand. Leah was not here. The Commander did not have her; that much was clear, although he was still seeking her. The alien woman was safe, at least from the officer of the Crowns. It was Thiele herself who was in immediate danger. The four men-at-arms had quietly surrounded her. She was, in effect, a prisoner, and for the moment she could do nothing about it.

With one gauntleted hand, the Commander indicated an open meadow a little way along the road. "There," he said.

The little knot of riders bore Thiele and Beast back with them. In the center of the meadow they stopped. Jardis, Alidon, and the brothers retreated in four separate directions to the distance of discretion, just beyond earshot and close-range sending. The Commander remained with Thiele.

It would be useless to try to run, she decided. An ornit could outspeed a kurval over short distances, but as soon as Beast became winded, they would catch her. No, she would have to rely on cunning and her special skills, although something told her the Commander would not be so easily taken off guard the second time; however, it would soon be dark.

"Where is she?" he demanded without preamble.

It was too late to pretend she did not know who he was talking about. He had felt her sending before he had seen her. He must know whom she had expected to find.

"Your Honor, I do not know," Thiele replied, momentarily glad this was true. She was free to project every digit of sincerity she could muster.

Suddenly, a realization came to her, a puzzle that had been worrying a corner of her mind beyond the fears of the immediate moment. She had expected to find Leah. She had felt Leah's own emanations, but they were not hers—they were the Commander's and so like Leah's that the two of them might have been identical twins. The Commander? And Leah? Was it possible? They were not even the same species, let alone the same gender.

He fingered the handle of his whip, but there was something jerky and mechanical in the habitual gesture. Thiele became aware of an agitation of mind, which he tried to suppress, and saw a haunted intensity in his eyes, which looked *through* rather than *at* her. She had thought him a bereaved singleton, yet her training told her he was in the throes of a twinship crisis. Very interesting! Perhaps he was driven to hunt Leah for reasons that had nothing to do with duty.

"She must be found," he hissed. "It is Crowns' business."

"She must return to her people," Thiele informed him quietly.

His eyes burned with a kind of terrified exaltation. "Her people! What do you know of her people?"

Thiele kept her own gaze steady, projecting sanity, reasonableness, calmness. She was making a second discovery about the Commander. Deeply ingrained in him was that body of belief called the Old Faith by the people of Oshune. It was a faith that one of Thiele's upbringing must respect, for her people were in a position to know how much truth lay in it behind the ignorance and inevitable superstitious nonsense.

What did it do to a man to discover himself twinned with one of his gods? One thing was sure: if Thiele's guess was correct, if there was some kind of twinship between him and Leah, he was unlikely to kill Leah or to allow her to be put to death if he could stop it. Whatever Leah's existence meant to him professionally or theologically, it would be a great personal agony to him if she should die. The Blessed did not murder their own twins, and the Commander had already been once through the trauma of that greatest loss.

"She needs her people," Thiele told him. "She will die unless she can rejoin them."

"Die?" He seemed to pull himself together. "She is injured?"

"Yes…."

"Badly?"

"I do not know. This world is not healthy for…."

"And you left her!" he accused.

She did not answer.

Again he seemed to take hold of himself. His men watched impassively. "You say, 'this world' as if it is not hers also. You spoke of her people," he said. "Have you seen them?"

Thiele sighed. "Not with my own eyes, your Honor."

"Do you know where they are?"

"No, your Honor." Assuming was not knowing, and even her assumptions were imprecise. It was a very *large* moon, after all.

"Do you know who they are?" The kurval sidestepped nervously as his hand tightened on the reins. "Tell me! She must have told you."

She lowered her eyes. There was nothing to be gained by trying to conceal Leah's origin from the Commander. He already half knew. He required only some kind of verification. All his life he had been waiting for this visitation, prepared to believe in it when it came. He was a dangerous man, but it was not in his interest to be an immediate threat to Leah's safety. And he was not Valad. Thiele began to allow herself a tiny hope. She raised her head and looked the Commander in the eyes.

"She is Starborn," she told him.

"So!" He let out his breath, and the wildness seemed to go with it. Suddenly the four soldiers were riding toward her. Their whips were out. There was no time to run. Their steeds could overtake Beast in a matter of oons.

Matvar was all iron again, controlled, merciless. "We require your assistance, Learned One," he said coldly. "You will take us to the place where you last saw our missing guest."

"Your Honor, she is not there." Under cloaking emotion Thiele thought of Ryl, of Akashtai. On no account would she betray them. She would have to convince the Commander that she had left Leah in some other place. The hut? It was far off, but it was the only place she could think of that she could lie about convincingly. She had been there with Leah. And the hut was away from Ryl's house and Akashtai's. It would mean making up for lost distance when she escaped, but that could not be helped. The bandits might have returned; that might distract these men just long enough. She would escape somehow. She must. If only Akashtai and that grandchild of hers had the sense to keep Leah away from the road. "She is not there," she repeated, allowing a tinge of deception to shade her voice and emanations.

"Nevertheless you will take us there," Matvar said.

There was nothing to be done about it. The hut would have to serve. There were five of them against her and Beast. Still, darkness was coming. "Very well, your Honor," said Thiele with a suggestion of a whine. "But it is very far away. A day's ride. I do not even know if I could find the place again."

"Perhaps we can assist your memory," Matvar said. He smiled unpleasantly. "Ride!"

The night was half gone when Matvar decided to stop. The men were weary. He himself would soon be unable to ignore his growing exhaustion. There must be a time to rest or else this woman of the Learned People would be able to play her tricks on them. She rode leaning against the scruffy neck of her ornit, as if half-asleep. He did not trust her.

They found a place off the road in the lee of some high rocks near a trickling brook. The yellow face of the Great Moon hung low in the sky. A light wind shivered the golden lace and blew dry winter leaves across the road. The woman seemed grateful to dismount. She let the ornit drink at the stream and led it to a patch of thick rhizo near the rock. She lay down, turned her back on the men, and drew her coat over herself.

Matvar appointed Alidon to stand guard over her and Raspid to watch Alidon, a little distance away. He considered tying the Learned One up, but he did not think ropes could hold her if she worked her spells on his men. Besides, there were tales here in the country that ill consequences visited those who treated Learned People with undue harshness. Instead, he hobbled the ornit and fastened its rope to one of the kurvals. The woman ignored him. Her beast stared at him coldly but seemed more interested in nibbling on the foliage than in maintaining its freedom. The kurvals would also keep watch. Their minds did not bend easily to any control but that of their own masters. As with his other two men, he prepared to sleep.

It was well past sunrise when Thiele awoke, cursing herself. How could she have fallen asleep? She had only meant to wait until the guards became inattentive enough to allow her to work upon them one at a time. She had missed her best chance to escape. What would become of her now? And of Leah?

If she had had any reason to think him capable, she would have suspected that Commander of paying her back for what she had done to him at the inn. But no, it was her own fault and, she realized ruefully, the betrayal of her body. No sleep for days, and on top of that....

Palmo! she thought sadly. *I should have been nearly home by now.*

Cautiously, she sat up and peered around the edge of her coat. Four of the men sat around a small fire while the fifth attended to the kurvals. Beast cropped rhizo in a leisurely manner, regarding her out of one large eye. The Commander gave her a long look and then turned away. Thiele was surprised to see what an attractive man he was. She hadn't noticed it at the inn; last night it had been getting dark, and she had been in fear for her life and....

Oh, Pestilence! she thought. I'm further along than I expected, if that one looks good to me. Well, let us hope they take no notice for awhile.

She got to her feet and brushed the crushed rhizo florets off her coat. She checked on Beast to make sure the rope hadn't hurt his ankle. The men politely kept their backs turned while she went to the stream and took care of her own needs. When she came to the fire, they offered her porridge and dried wineberries, which she accepted. They gave no sign of being aware of her impending fertility, although it was early yet. She thought she could control her emanations enough to conceal her condition for another day, but she knew she would not be able to suppress the pheromones for long. What a miserable complication!

Matvar gave the Learned One no opportunity to escape as the party rode south. He did not understand why she had not made the attempt, especially last night, when his own forces were vulnerable. He was beginning to think she might be less involved in the escape of the Sky Dweller than he had supposed. Had she not been searching also? She had been cooperative, considering the way he had treated her. She was a comely female, too. Quite remarkably pretty, in fact. He hadn't noticed before. Valad had noticed, according to regional gossip.

Thiele had to admit to herself she felt much better for the rest. After they passed the ancient crossroads with its bare-picked ruins, she felt almost euphoric and not all of it could be credited to her condition. There was no chance now they would come face to face with Akashtai and Leah, which was a great burden off her mind. Either Akashtai had been delayed and had not yet come so far east as the crossroad, or she had used another path. If anyone knew how to get through that haunted region of the wild, she did. Most people who ventured into that part of the forest came out of it mad, if they ever reappeared at all.

She sensed that the mood of the Commander toward herself had begun to change. She did her best to encourage it, engaging him in polite conversation several times during the afternoon. This was not easy; he was a man of few words. It was difficult balancing social warmth against the fight to repress the emanations of her fertility. As the sun fell towards the west, he seemed to become preoccupied and twice failed to answer when she addressed him. The other men were beginning to watch her with greater alertness, although she did not yet detect any consciousness in them of her condition. She was running out of time. Soon they would arrive at the hut. If she played them right, they might let her go then. If not, she must, she absolutely must, get away from them after dark.

They came to the hut at twilight and disturbed a small party of bandits, who fled into the forest in several directions, and left miscellaneous booty of little value and a haunch of loper half-roasted over the fire. They made no attempt to face the soldiers, and there was no moment when they occupied much of Matvar's attention.

There was, as Thiele had foretold, no sign of the alien. South, south, south, thought Thiele, as she had been thinking loudly for the past several kroons. She must have gone south, back to the vehicle she came from. Thiele created a little cloud of conviction around her: South, definitely south. She must have gone south, and it has nothing to do with me. I'm of no use now. In fact, I am absolutely a hindrance.

"East," said Matvar, breaking a long silence. His usual grayish color had deepened almost to lavender. "She went east from here."

The soldiers and Thiele looked at him. Suddenly Thiele was afraid again.

"She is east of here. She is not alone. They are going east, I think."

Ryl? Thiele wondered. East? Why east? Why can his Honor reach Leah now when he couldn't all day? Doesn't he care I might guess his secret?

"Your Honor," she ventured. "I have brought you to the place as I promised. It seems you now have no further need of my guidance, and I have certain devotional exercises I must attend to. Will you give me leave to be on my way?"

Each one of the men, separately, shifted his stance. She felt their eyes on her, felt them look away again. If she got away, it would be none too soon. Matvar dragged his attention back to her. "Dine with us first," he commanded, gesturing toward the half-cooked meal. To her own considerable surprise, Thiele found herself accepting his invitation without protest.

"Learned One, are you acquainted with the magistrate of this district?"

Matvar watched her face grow pale as he asked the question. Her emanations shrank. It was interesting that she feared Valad more than him. It was interesting that she had stayed to share their windfall feast, obviously against her own better judgment. He was now quite sure of it. The woman was fertile, although she tried desperately to conceal that fact. She had been blooming under their eyes all day. Well, if she was keeping herself for someone or intending to avoid conception, she had nothing to fear from the armsmen of the Kings.

"Yes, your Honor. I am acquainted with Veen Valad. I…I have been his guest."

"My sympathies." Matvar smiled less coldly than usual. He had sent his men outside the hut to keep watch or tend to the animals and equipment, so the two of them were alone.

"I have cause to believe," he continued, "that his lordship has another guest at the moment. I believe he has the one we are looking for."

Thiele stared at him. "That is bad news, your Honor. But, begging your pardon, how do you know?" *What could have happened,* she wondered.

He looked at the fire. "I have received information. I intend to relieve him of this responsibility."

"I see," said Thiele, who didn't quite. Her thoughts whirled. If Valad had indeed got hold of Leah somehow, it was much worse than the Commander catching her. Valad had no personal interest in keeping the alien alive. In fact, if he realized what she was, his politics would demand her instant death and the destruction of her body. If he did not realize what she was, his disgust at her appearance might prompt him to do any number of unspeakable things to Leah. But why would he take her prisoner at all? Why would he bother? Suddenly she thought of a reason.

"His lordship has a second estate east of here," Matvar went on. "He is taking her in that direction, although they have stopped moving, perhaps for the night. He has more men than I, and in any case, we could not overtake them before he is within his own hedges."

"He will not let you in," said Thiele. "If he knows you want her…."

"He knows!"

"He will not let you anywhere near her."

"True."

"Unless I am with you," she heard herself say. "I could get in easily, but I might not be able to get her out."

"I hoped you would understand, Learned One. You see, I can get her out. I could get you out also, unless you choose to stay."

Thiele made a disgusted noise in her throat. "And what then, Commander?"

He shrugged. "You tell me she is hurt. My duty will be clearer when I see her condition. I give my word she will come to no harm from me. Neither will you, if you give me your help."

"If I refuse?"

"In that case, I can give you no assurances of any kind. And the…one we seek will remain in custody of the Magistrate."

Thiele took a deep breath. It was possible this man was lying to her, that he had no idea where Leah was, or that he planned to abandon her, Thiele, to Valad's mercies in trade for the alien. She was inclined to think he was telling the truth. She would have been able to detect traces of a purposeful deception, and there was no reason for him to fabricate such a tale unless he meant to entice her into Valad's clutches. That was possible, but considering the Commander's unconcealed contempt for Valad, it was unlikely he would put himself out to do the Magistrate's little errands. Nor was he likely to trade her for Leah, Thiele thought with wry amusement. Even if he now intended to do so, he would change his mind by then. There were advantages to being a female in the fertile phase.

Thiele realized that she had no choice. To untwin herself from Leah's plight at this point would be wrong. She must find out what had happened, whether Ryl or Akashtai had been exposed. She must know whether Leah had really been taken by Valad. She must honor her pledge of friendship. And it was certainly true that she had a better chance of getting away again in the company of armed men than she would on her own, not to mention what it would be like with Leah weak and still injured. "Very well, your Honor," she said at last. "I will do it."

"Good." He stood up. "We ride at dawn. You may sleep in here. You will not be disturbed." He gave her a courteous salute and went out into the darkness, closing the rickety door behind him. She heard him muttering something to the man on watch outside.

For several oons she was actually sorry he had gone. For several oons more she chastised herself for even thinking such thoughts. She went to the window on the shadow side of the hut. It was a little too small to climb through without making noise. There was a man on guard anyway and probably another somewhere watching him. It didn't matter. The timing of all of this was ludicrous. In a very bad temper, she laid out her bedroll in the cleanest corner of the hut and composed herself for sleep.

NEW MACHINERY

The answer to the flawed silicon flake came at last in a dream. Koriam sat by a river, his head aching, and his computer in ruins behind him. A gray waterslider surfaced for a moment in front of him, then ducked beneath the wave again, sleeking its fur in the running stream. A burrnut caught on its tail was pulled free.

"Clean!" said Koriam, sitting up in bed, and remembered the byword, Clean as a Starborn. His headache was gone. He pulled the blanket around him, wishing he'd thought to take another the night before. But perhaps it was not so much the morning chill on his bones as it was his own excitement. If he couldn't find a fault in the pattern of the flakes, it must be because there wasn't one to find. He must have slipped somehow in molding the flake— reached under the head muffler to scratch his hair, or not checked the laundering of his slippers and robe. Or something. At least, he hoped that was it.

He made up the bed and headed in the pink morning light for the wash-tubs. He built a fire under one and left the water to heat while he went and took his work-clothes from the laboratory. At the same time, he called to his assistants on the project to come help. It involved a little juggling of schedules, but after consultation with Verret, they worked it out. For good measure Koriam took down the clothesline and pins, and added them to the laundry, too.

In the afternoon, their clean clothes still a little damp and smelling of lye, they set about making a fresh set of flakes, crystallizing a batch of silicon to make tiny ingots and slicing the ingots thin.

Koriam's absorption was marred only by awareness of Palmo. His twin, still upset at the order to turn off the sound-senders, was obsessed, imagining over and over, a picture of himself walking into the sound-chamber, turning on the sound-pick, and sending sounds. In his imagination, the operators in the room did not notice him. When Koriam realized what it was, he gave out a protest. Palmo sent back a "sorry," and either stopped doing it or at least blocked it off.

Although the operators on duty did not know who was making the disturbance, they had caught the invasive picture. When Koriam left the laboratory near sunset, he found the operators standing formal guard by the door instead of trusting to a mental watch on their surroundings. They had requested arms from Verret and were clutching at long-barreled guns. One guard had been an aristocrat before joining the Brokers of Knowledge, and was unconsciously trying to hold her whip ready in one hand. She did not entirely trust the odd new weapons the Brokers had.

Both guards started to tell him their worries, but Koriam interrupted. "It's just Palmo. I told him to stop. But you're right, there's no harm standing guard for a while." He rubbed at his chin. "Tell you what, if I ask to go in and check the equipment or whatever—don't let me." He didn't think Palmo could imitate his thoughts well enough to fool a careful observer, but the physical resemblance could be misleading in some circumstances, and it would be just as well to forestall the possibility. He couldn't think of any reason he would need to go in the sound-chamber, so he wouldn't be hurting anything by keeping himself out. He thought about suggesting that whips weren't needed on duty, but decided the idea would strike her as an insult.

Koriam opened his mind and showed his brother what had just occurred.

"Sorry," Palmo thought back. "I didn't realize I was thinking so loud."

"Just don't think about turning on the sound-senders."

"I *can't* not. I think it's what ought to be done, and I can't help thinking it."

"You're not planning to try a stunt like that, are you?"

Palmo thought a kind of snorting thought, a mixture of indignation and laughter. "I wasn't, but now that you mention it—"

"Palmo!"

"Just because I'd like to walk straight in doesn't mean I think I can do it." He thought of a tangle of santik blown flat in the wind and a draft of sweetness rising from the little green flowers. It was an image that did duty for an apologetic sigh.

Koriam joined in the wind.

The remembered purple leaves bent to remembered ground, sprang up, and grew still.

"Can't help thinking," Palmo said, "but I promise I'll be quieter."

Koriam wished he could be a waterslider with nothing to worry about but his next meal and clean fur. Of course, a waterslider would still have sex to worry about, wouldn't it? And hunters. Even so…. He pushed the image to the back of his mind and went looking for his own supper.

For some days there seemed to be nothing to worry about except silicon flakes and other people's computers. Koriam would have preferred to think about the silicon flakes full-time while others were imprinting them with diagrams and hooking the flakes up to the input/output wires, but the implementation details were both useful and absorbing, too.

A batch of equipment from Thiele turned up, although Thiele herself was not with it. Kron and a woman from the Forest Dwellers brought it. They had a wild story to tell—they said Thiele had found a Starborn woman, and they said she said they must turn on the sound-senders to tell the Starborn's people. Kron hadn't talked to Thiele or the stranger himself. Angin had, but her memories seemed to be mixed up with dreams about Jumpers. And Thiele had lost the Starborn she claimed to have found. Angin thought she ought to go south again to look for the stranger, and Kron offered to guide her, but Koriam asked them to stay. He thought Angin's story might grow clearer—in spite of the tangled dreams—and more convincing on better acquaintance;

perhaps Kron's memories could help Angin sort her own. Palmo was quick to second this argument, and Angin and Kron agreed to try. Gradually, some were convinced, but more were cautious and said they should not go jumping cliff to abyss. Word might come from Thiele or one of the others in the area. Koriam worried about the delay and Palmo's fretting, but then he was caught up by his work again and half forgot.

As computers were restored and made operational, his expertise was needed to help figure out how they worked. They had a collection of manuals, but the manuals never seemed to match the particular models their scavenging brought them. Paper did not last as well as components, but between the library from the time the group began and the rare archives turned up by the search, they had a reasonable hoard. (In ancient legend, there were giant snowslaens on the ice floes, invulnerable to weapons, with hoards of diamonds in their icy lairs. Verret sometimes claimed the hoards were really an allegory of libraries, but hedged when asked what she meant by reality.) Scribes made fresh copies of the old ones and painstakingly collated them for errors against the originals. Sometimes the originals had errors, too.

Verret's skill at finding things she wanted to be able to do with computers had the drawback—or the advantage, depending on how you looked at it—of exposing the areas of ignorance and understanding, whether it was coaxing a visual instruction-set to draw in perspective or hunting for primes.

Koriam stuck a stack of manuals in a case on a morning when the sun had decided to show up again after days of steady, gray rain, and set out by himself to brood over them. If he stared at the instructions long enough, maybe he could match up some of the diagrams with some of the newly-arrived equpment or with some of the models they already had. Or they might give him ideas to try on the stubborn isolates. Or he might get a match next time an agent came in.

He went downhill instead of up, for the change, and along the aisle that had once been a road. A velvety mat of dark red rhizo had covered up the paving centuries ago, with here and there a patch of yellow firn in the sunny spots. In some places, especially further south toward the nearest farms, the old road was occasionally blocked with fallen trees or rocks, but the ancient construction could not have been hidden along the whole of its length, at least not without a technology equal to the one their ancestors had lost.

A double row of bheshwood trees still gave shade in the summer to those who knew their way past the obstructions. The trees came late into leaf so far north, but the shining black flowers were out, hanging in little streamers from the branches and giving off a quiet, soapy sort of smell. Beyond was the natural forest, mostly birka trees, with some resin trees. The little yellow birka leaves, brighter than firn, were coming out over the purple wood. On the resin trees, soft new needles showed brassy against the old bronze.

Koriam walked a long way before settling down to his manuals—for exercise, and for the pleasure of it. Sometimes he had to detour around a clump of poisonous wirethorn, and a few shuteyes had already started buzzing around to be slapped at. Shuteyes aside, everything there to see or sniff or touch was a delight to him, and the delight seemed far more than he remembered. It was so much keener than usual that Koriam decided he had been working and worrying too much. He should take walks more often. How that was to be done without overloading Verret or some of the others was a problem. No, it wasn't. They were all doing too much and should simply do less of it. And go for walks more often. Except some of them didn't like walks. Well, they could take up music. Or something.

Once he startled a few big purple dromils almost as large as bosorns, as they leaned out from between the bheshwood trees to munch on the rhizo. They tossed their heads at him, showing off the coils of their long horns, but he kept walking forward, too slowly to let them think they needed to stand and fight off an attack, too firmly to look like something to be threatened. They snorted, backed a pace, and vanished in the shadows of the forest.

When he came to a rockfall blocking the road, he sat down on a conveniently-sized granite boulder and rested his hands on the rock. It was not until he looked at a manual and felt confused by his first glance at the text that he realized that he was not alone.

His delight in the outing was, in fact, exactly twice what it should have been.

"Get out!" he yelled, trying to close himself off.

Palmo's body had gone through the motions he had rehearsed obsessively in imagination—walking up to the sound-chamber, waiting until the operators were absorbed in conversation and not looking at the door. In he walked, all his conscious mind smelling bheshwood streamers with Koriam and not a thought within-doors to catch the operators' attention until Koriam started his hullabaloo.

Palmo turned the sound-picks on, beaming out a steady signal. He even had time to say, "Hello, hello! Are you there? H—" before anything happened.

It felt like a hill of rocks collapsing on them. It fell again, and again, and kept falling. Koriam knew by the change in his muscles that they were trying to lift their arms to hold the hill back. Then they knew nothing.

LEAH'S DREAM

Leah was stretched out on a large, wooden storage chest in a small room of Valad's northern mansion, wondering if the door would open again. It had, twice. Once, a guard pushed in a wooden box with a washbasin on top. Leah had opened the panel on the side when the guard had gone and discovered a pottery contrivance inside that had an obvious use. She closed the box hastily—there were herbs hanging from a corner giving the box a stale perfumed smell.

The next time the guard had thrown in a few blankets. She had made a bed on the chest's padded top, but it was hard to sleep despite her fatigue. Would the door open again? She watched it nervously as the light dimmed in the room.

Before sunset, she had checked the window as a possible exit, but it was several meters above the ground, with no ledge or landing. No, if there was to be an escape, it had to be through that door. More important, someone would have to rescue her—she moved far too slowly in comparison with these people to make a run for it. She wondered how long it would be before Thiele could send aid. There was no doubt in Leah's mind that she would; Thiele gave a pledge of friendship which seemed to involve her personal honor. But could help arrive before Valad did who-knows-what to her? And if Thiele came back, could she free her, Leah, and escape Valad as well?

Leah was afraid for Thiele. Although her telepathic abilities were still largely untrained, she could pick up distinctly that Valad was obsessed with her. Leah he paid little attention to, other than as a way to get Thiele to him. He seemed to think Leah was from a certain area of the planet known for mutant births—Leah couldn't decide whether the place was radioactive, an old toxic waste dump, or what.

She closed her eyes. Even so, she could sense the presence of the guard standing outside the locked door. He, too, seemed to have no interest in her. She hoped it stayed that way. With the keys, he could enter whenever he wished. She didn't think she could fight him off if he tried to rape her. No... better not to think such things. He might pick up her thoughts, get ideas. Think about something else.

Her mind wandered to the space station. Didn't they know she had crashed? Weren't they looking for her? And Topaz and Diamond—where were *they?* Perhaps it was foolish of her to keep hoping they were following her, staying in the concealment of the woods. She had heard the sounds of something large in the brush often enough, but was it the Querlitzen? Could they keep up with her pace if they had had nothing but water to ingest since then? They wouldn't starve in so short a time, but with only the brains of the two of them linked together, she wondered if they would know how to be careful while sampling things to eat. How could they find nourishment, and how could they keep running so far and so fast if they didn't? And how long would it take to track them down if they were lost? Would anyone find them? For that matter, would anyone find her? It was beginning to seem unlikely.

Dozing, she found images forming in her mind. Thiele walked in front of her, in corridors familiar to her because Valad's men had brought her through them earlier. She could not read Thiele's mind, though she sensed her confidence. There was a tingling sensation in her nose. Thiele gave off a pleasant, sexually stimulating odor. She did her best to ignore it.

Servants opened the intricately carved doors to Valad's study. He stood in the middle of the room, dressed exactly as he had been when Leah had last seen him. Why are those clothes familiar to me? she thought, then her concentration was broken by Valad's voice.

"Ah, Commander, so you have brought my beloved to me at last!" He sighed passionately, then fell to the floor at Thiele's feet. Thiele looked over to her with an expression of mock resignation. (Why could she identify an expression she had never seen before?) When Valad stood again, Thiele gestured at him invitingly. He took her hand.

"Well, Commander, for once you have been useful to me. Name your reward. If it is reasonable, you shall have it." He added dryly, "I, too, have been useful. Your fugitive has come into my keeping. Tomorrow, as Crowns Magistrate, I will examine her. Or," he added wickedly, "perhaps the day after."

"She is *my* prisoner!"

"She is the Crowns' prisoner. But you deserve a fair reward, Commander. What will you have?"

"Two kurvals would be sufficient, Magistrate..." (what was a kurval?) "... if you could spare them, and saddles as well."

"Done," said Valad. He motioned, presumably to one of the servants; she heard footsteps retreating behind her. He turned to a tray on a low table. Five glasses and a jeweled decanter rested on it. Two of the glasses had been already filled. Valad poured a third, then offered it to her. "Come, let us all drink," he said. "This is a day for rejoicing."

He smiled at Matvar. "You will not have heard the news," he continued. "Mine are not the only nuptials pending. Their Majesties are to be married. I have the honor of being cousin to the brides."

Leah felt herself stiffening. "Your uncle's daughters, Magistrate? They are children!"

"Old enough." Valad's smile broadened. "So you see you have brought my beloved to me at a most auspicious time. Let us drink to their Majesties' lifelong happiness. And to you, Commander, in parting; to you, beloved, for what is to come."

Stunned, Matvar sipped as Valad turned to take another glass. He found the taste at once pleasantly familiar and strangely sour. Leah pursed her lips in her sleep. Over the rim of his glass, Matvar thought he saw Valad hesitate, as if wondering which of the remaining two glasses to take next. But why bother, if they were identical? Perhaps they were not. Matvar let another small sip remain on his tongue for a moment to be sure it was not drugged. Satisfied, he swallowed. He hoped Thiele was wise enough to be similarly cautious.

Valad offered a glass to Thiele. "It is good that you have finally seen the wisdom of the Veen beliefs. I am pleased."

Matvar suppressed the urge to wince. The wisdom of the Veen, indeed!

Compliantly, Thiele accepted the glass from Valad, sniffed it, appeared to sip, taste, and swallow it, as one did with any fine vintage. Valad watched her with a glee that Matvar found alarming as he gulped down the contents of his own glass. Valad then asked Matvar of news of his patrol, but seemed only half-interested in Matvar's answers—he rarely took his eyes off Thiele.

When Matvar had finished his report (how did I know all that?), Thiele reached into her carry pouch. Before she could open her hand, Valad grabbed it and pried it open. Thiele did not resist. Matvar peered at the contents of her palm. They seemed to be common sweet drops. Valad laughed.

"Would you like some candy?" Thiele asked. Her voice sounded strangely high-pitched.

Valad gestured a polite refusal. (Is that what it was?) Thiele ate a piece, then held out her hand in Matvar's direction. Matvar also declined to take one. Slowly, she put her hand back into her pouch. As she brought it out again, she stumbled, clutching at Valad as if for balance. He lowered her into a chair. She slumped, eyelids fluttering. Matvar strode forward to attempt a direct mind-touch. Her thoughts were unfocused and weak.

"You gave her *tinte*," said Matvar to Valad.

Valad was kneeling by the chair. He turned to look up at Matvar. "Naturally. I do not want her to have the opportunity to leave again." When Matvar continued to stare, shocked, he added, "You may go now."

There was nothing else to do, not with Valad's servants and guards about. The last thing he saw as the hall steward closed the door was Valad removing Thiele's boots.

Matvar dawdled around the hallways, stopping to retie his boots, moving on when the servants began to eye him suspiciously. What was he to do? This was not part of the plan. (Plan?) Thiele might not recover from the tinte until sunrise; if Valad was as brutal as his reputation, Thiele might not be able to leave even when she did recover from the drug's effects. (In her sleep, Leah shuddered at the image of what Thiele might look like come morning.)

What was he to do? The kings were to marry the daughters of Lord Veen. It was a great triumph for the Veen family and their faction and a terrible blow to all true believers of the Old Faith. How had the old man done it? What was happening in the City? Was it all over? Matvar wondered what his chances were of getting into Oshune alive with the Sky Dweller. Suppose the two of them survived as far as the Cathedral, what then?

He passed a deserted parlor. He could see the inside dimly because of the double moonlight through the windows. Here he might wait unobserved for some time. His men, (my men?) he knew, would have better excuse for the delay—they had to wait until he returned, and who knew how long Valad might entertain him? In time he began to doze; in his sleep he dreamed of the Sky Dwellers: fantastic beings, singing high-pitched melodies, gliding through metal hallways, swimming in the air. Metal ships that sailed the black waters among bright points of light. A green-blue-white sphere; an orange-yellow-blue-white sphere. The Star Ship he had found in the clearing, whole, approaching cloud tops. Then...

A sound startled him. Instantly awake, he turned to the door to see Thiele silhouetted there. She shuffled forward, then sank into the couch beside him, hand on forehead.

Matvar turned back to the door. "Where is Valad?"

"Sleeping the sleep of the dead."

"You did not kill him?"

"No. He was working his way up from my feet when the antidote began to take effect. By the time his kisses reached my knees, he was too deeply involved in his lovemaking to notice my reaching to his sleep center. He will not become self-aware again until sunrise." She put her hand down. "There. The headache is gone. I'm recovering quickly."

"That was not candy."

"It was not." She reached for Matvar's pack. "Let me change clothes now, and we can find Leah."

"She is nearby. I can feel her (twin)touch on my mind."

Thiele's mental powers had come back strongly enough for her to pick up the unspoken thought. She pretended not to notice since it seemed to embarrass Matvar. It explained a great deal.

Thiele stripped to her underwear. Matvar turned his head. She redressed in the clothes of a soldier of Matvar's troop, then stuffed her own clothes in Matvar's pack.

She tapped his shoulder. "Ready. Let's go."

Leah stirred, opened her eyes, and lifted her head. There were two squares of moonlight on the floor. She sighed. Eyes open, she lay down again. A wish-fulfillment dream: she wanted a rescue, so she dreamed of it. No one was really coming to rescue her. The despair of that thought was so sharp she almost cried. She dared not. She did not want to give the guard an excuse to come in. Besides, she was tired. She'd gotten too little sleep since coming to this planet, far too little. She abandoned herself to the exhaustion.

In her dream, she watched as Thiele approached the guard—her guard—from the side. A touch to the neck; the guard's face went blank, though he blinked normally. Thiele withdrew her hand.

"So, it was *you* who affected my guard at the inn," Matvar whispered, astonished.

Thiele acknowledged with a movement of the eyebrow as she slipped the keys from the guard's belt. She opened the door, and saw....

Someone shook Leah's shoulder. She looked up to see Thiele's face in the moonlight, keys in her hand. Thiele was dressed in a uniform. Matvar stood behind her. Leah sat up. "I'm still dreaming," she murmured.

"No," said Thiele. Matvar handed her his pack. "You must dress in these clothes and follow us," she added, pulling out a shirt and pants. "Then we leave."

Leah still suspected she was dreaming, but was more than willing to give Thiele the benefit of the doubt. With Thiele's help, she changed. Matvar turned his back to them. Thiele stuffed Leah's own clothes back into the pack. "Come now. He will walk slowly, so we can keep up. Slouch as well as you can, and keep your cap close to your face. They've dimmed the lamps, and there are few servants about. Say nothing, and we can escape here without anyone suspecting."

When they were out the door, Thiele locked it and replaced the keys. As promised, Matvar walked slowly; what few servants spied them did not give them a second glance. They walked out of the house and into a stableyard where some men slumped by riding animals. One started as they came close and aroused the others. "The stars smile on fools," he muttered.

"You have the extra mounts?" asked Matvar.

One of the men pointed.

"Won't they notice the difference?" asked Leah of Thiele as Thiele boosted her into the saddle.

"No," said Thiele. "*If* they counted us as we came in, and if the same guards are there to count us as we go out, and if they reckon there are more of us going out, they will simply think that Valad has loaned an additional man or two to the Commander while he is in the district."

Clinging to the reins, feet in the stirrups, Leah managed to ride out with the others as if she knew what she was doing. She heard no alarm raised behind them.

NORTH AGAIN

It was growing light. A thin mist grayed the forest and condensed in heavy dew upon the ruins. There were sounds from all sides—the gurgling whistles of wheedlers and the gentle call of a jingler, like a ringing of phantom bells.

Matvar stood near the little fire, gazing into the flames. Now and then he glanced across it at the Starborn woman, who slumped wearily against the remains of wall. She had returned the uniform parts to their owners but still wore the coat, Matvar's own, wrapped around her in the morning chill. Her eyes were closed. She was aware of his gaze but did not acknowledge it.

They had reached an equilibrium, fragile still but strengthening. She seemed to understand the need to keep a distance between them while they learned each other and built modes of understanding. For Matvar, this was not entirely a matter of rebuilding, no matter how twin-like she was. The private system of codes he had shared with Rudvar was no longer appropriate; most of the old symbols were meaningless to her. Some she rejected. She had symbols of her own, too, strange linked images that no longer inspired fear and disgust in him. She did not press them on him. Indeed, she had already learned to veil her thoughts from him. They were left with their shared exhaustion, embarrassment, and grief: an awareness of presence.

They had ridden all night. The Learned One, who knew this country well, had led them in a long arc southeast of Valad's place, crossing the road and winding down to a tributary of the river Angin, where they had turned west, wading the sandy shallows. They made only one brief stop to pick up the Learned One's riding Ornit, which had been left tied to a tree. A cut to the northwest brought them back to the road not far from the ancient crossroads. Here they sheltered amid the dead leavings of the Old Times. The Starborn woman was deeply interested in the place. The size of it impressed her. She desired to dig. Matvar could not fathom why. There was nothing of value here.

The Learned One approached through the trees. Two of the men were with her, the brothers. The three of them had taken the animals to water. Their talk was very lively, although she had made it entirely clear as soon as they had ridden free from Valad's hedges that she was promised to someone and unavailable for courting. Still, she plainly enjoyed the enhancement of her emanations and the male attention it brought, now that she was reassured that the men would honor her commitment. She raised her head and laughed at something Haspar said. From the campfire Jardis and Alidon watched her approach with eagerness. The Starborn woman opened her eyes.

Jardis took two sticks and maneuvered a steaming can away from the edge of the fire. He dipped a cupful of sourstrap tea and offered it to the Learned One.

"Thank you," she said. She smiled at him. She faced Matvar and said, "Remember what I offered you. There is a place, if you choose." She took the cup and turned. They watched her carry it across the tumbled stones to where the stranger sat. Haspar sighed audibly. He was young.

Matvar accepted the next cup of the brew and gestured to the others to help themselves. He remembered. She offered nothing that would have attracted the man he had been five days ago, little more than her belief that the returning Sky Dwellers would come to her people and not to Oshune. She had spoken so guardedly of her own people and homeland that he still could not decide if they maintained the Old Faith or followed some heresy of their own. Even the day before, he would have refused to listen in spite of his growing attraction to the Learned One. Since then, he had received bad news and he had spent a night in proximity to his Starborn twin. Her needs were now known to him and no longer separable from his. The alternatives were both unpalatable, but he knew his choice was already made.

He waited for the men to settle themselves with their drinks. He gathered their attention. Reluctantly, they dragged their eyes away from Thiele, who lingered with the Sky Dweller, talking softly near the fallen wall.

"It is time to return," he said.

The brothers exchanged glances. Jardis narrowed his eyes. Alidon coughed.

Matvar was silent for a moment. "You know what she is," he said at last. There was no need to tell them which "she" he meant. "I have told you what has happened in the City. The Magistrate did not lie. The Learned One knows him well. He was telling the truth."

They believed and understood.

"I am not going back with you."

They stared at him, Thiele's charms momentarily forgotten.

"She will not survive away from her own people," he continued. "The Learned One knows how she can be returned to them. I will do this."

"We will come with you, my lord," said Raspid. His brother gestured agreement. "We will come," echoed Alidon and Jardis.

"It is not permitted," Matvar answered without regret. "Agund Alidon," he said.

"My lord?"

"We are kin."

"That is my honor, my lord." Alidon stuttered a little.

"I require you to go to my father. Tell him what has happened. Tell him I live, but he may not see me again. Tell him—tell him They have returned."

Matvar made a prayer sign. The others did the same.

"I will do as you ask, my lord," Alidon said.

"Jardis, you will go with him?"

"I will. We will go quietly into the City, I think."

"That would be wise. Come back then to this province. You are not released from duty here. Raspid and Haspar, you will return to the inn today. Report to Arunesh, to Labek if he is recovered.

"Tell them I said this: Be courteous to the Magistrate. Cooperate with him no more than necessary. Tell him nothing. Keep things quiet. The inn is a good headquarters; they can carry on the routine work from there."

The twins bowed.

"Your report will not mention that we left the Magistrate's house with the women. We never saw them at all. If the Magistrate comes looking, you will know nothing. He will not know who was with me, and he has no authority to question any of the men. Guard your emanations."

"We will, my lord. What shall we tell of you?"

"Say I have gone back to the wrecked Star Ship. Say Alidon and Jardis have gone with me. You do not know why. We will rejoin the troop as soon as we can."

"You will return then, lord?"

"I do not know."

"This will make you feel warmer," Thiele said.

"I know. Thank you." Leah sipped the tea, grateful she could now trust a few of the foodstuffs here. "Why do they all watch you so closely?" she asked, then felt herself blushing. "Forgive me if the question is improper."

Thiele smiled. "If you were one of my people it would be no mystery to you. When a female of my species enters the phases of the year when she is capable of conceiving children, she changes. It…is very noticeable."

"Oh." Leah tried to decide whether she had noticed any change in Thiele in the seven (was it seven?) days since they had met. She decided she hadn't. Thiele seemed exactly the same to her. The men were definitely behaving differently, though. And *he* knew there was a change. She had suspected something of the sort. It would be interesting to ask Thiele about courtship practices of her species, but Leah had more important concerns.

"What will they do with me?" she asked.

"They intended to take you to the capital city on the south coast. You were to be exhibited before the royal court as evidence that the people from the stars had returned to this world. Such a return has been foretold by one of their religions and denied by another sect. The second lot seem to be in control at the moment, so you would be most unsafe there."

Leah nodded, forgetting the movement was meaningless to Thiele. *How the hell am I going to get out of this,* she wondered. *Five against two, and I can barely walk.*

"Do not give up hope," said Thiele. "I have been talking to the Commander. He has a good reason now not to return to the city. He has an even better reason to be watchful of your safety. I offered him a chance to ensure that, but I do not know what he will decide to do. Whatever happens, I will stay with you." She sent reassurance, a mental pat on the shoulder, and went back to the fire. The men greeted her enthusiastically.

Leah did not call her back to tell her they were not going to the city. She almost regretted it. A city! It would have been a fascinating experience.

She looked around at the ruins. There had once been a good-sized settlement here. She had seen evidence of building, long before they had got this far, and some of the structures had been quite massive. Time and the forest had worked on them too much for her to tell if this was a site of the old galactic culture or only an indigenous community. Ever since they had stopped she had been itching to do some digging. There wasn't time, and she hadn't the energy.

As near as she could tell after all that riding in the dark, this place was some distance west of Valad's house. She hoped they were far enough away. The ruins seemed an obvious place for anybody to come hunting fugitives, much too exposed. Thiele, though, did not seem worried about pursuit. Maybe the soldiers were guarantee against that.

Leah wondered how near they had come to the Western Forest. She tried to think again of her strange journey through the trees with the Jumpers, but it seemed even more blurred and dreamlike than it had at the time. As if it didn't want to be remembered. She would not trust herself to go back there. She hoped the chance would not be offered; she yearned for it.

Stranger still was this sensation of being double-minded, her odd rapport with *him*, the silvery man, the Commander. One couldn't call it an intimacy, although it could very easily grow to be that in time. And it wasn't like her communication with Thiele. Odd as that contact felt, it was very much as she had always imagined telepathic communication must be. Like talking to oneself, only there was another person, an actual Other, on the receiving end, and they were truly *there* in a way she couldn't describe in words.

The man, Matvar, was more *there* than even Thiele was when she was "thinking" to Thiele, only his presence had a different quality to it. The best mental image she could devise for it was as if she and he were joined together back to back or side by side, facing outward from each other and yet linked, while she and Thiele were face to face. Her link with the man reminded her of the closeness she had sometimes imagined existed between her and a lover in the early euphoric stages, but there was no such emotional content in this contact. A faint embarrassment, a good deal of caution, lingering surprise, a very worn and old grief, and resignation: she could no longer tell which of these feelings belonged to her and which came from the man.

As a sociologist she found it interesting that the emotions of this otherworld being were the least alien thing about him. Even after intensive training and years of working with aliens, she was still baffled on some fundamental level by the mentalities of the Jheehan, the Hultzu, the Querlitzen. There was no such barrier between her and the people of this world. She could imagine a very good working relationship between this species and her own, provided her mental contact with them was not unique. The Hultzu were going to be gravely annoyed.

She slept a little. When she awoke, the mist had burned away and the sun was well up. It was much warmer. She felt better.

The fire had been put out and there was no one in sight. She sensed the Commander somewhere nearby. As she stirred, Thiele came into her field of view leading Beast and one of the kurvals. It was still not easy for Leah to read the facial expressions of these people, but she could read Thiele's feelings, and Thiele was obviously pleased.

"Can you ride?" she asked in a low voice. "We are going. I am taking you home."

Leah stretched out her cramped arms and legs and got painfully to her feet, leaning on the stones for support. "What about the men?"

"The four have departed southward. Matvar is coming with us. "

Matvar. Before now Thiele had always referred to him as the Commander. "With us?" Leah repeated. "Why?"

"It's too far for twintouch," Thiele replied. "Even if you had a normal range. He says it is better than it was, but you were quite faint at two days' separation."

Leah looked at her. "I don't understand."

"He wants to stay in range," said Thiele, with an air of explaining the obvious.

"In range of what?"

"Of twintouch. With you."

"Twintouch. Is that what you call this, when you communicate from one mind to another?"

"No," said Thiele. "Only between twins. You are his twin. Come. We must ride." She boosted Leah onto the kurval.

Thiele's anxiety to be gone was so strong Leah decided to ask no more questions. She was puzzled by this use of the word "twin" to describe the kind of rapport she had with Matvar. Thiele seemed to be *meaning* "twin" in the ordinary sense, two people born together, and that did not make sense. Perhaps there would be an explanation eventually. All that really mattered now was that where they were going there would be a radio. She could get a shuttle down here, get this exhausting weight off her feet, get herself properly taken care of by medical. Have a proper bath. *Then* she would write a report. Justice, would she write a report!

From the crossroads, the three of them rode north. Leah did not recognize the land. Both her previous journeys in the north had been off the road they now followed. Matvar was quiet. She could still feel him, but somehow he had shut himself off from her. She could no longer detect his feelings. He continued to watch Thiele, but he seemed as much occupied with his private thoughts as he was with the attractions of a fertile female. Thiele was both weary and jubilant. She was now clearly the leader of the party. From time to time she pointed things out to Leah, identified a plant or animal or commented on the geology and climate.

"Now, those we call curledge," she said, gesturing toward a thicket of low, gnarled shrubs that grew along the margin of the road. Blue-purple leaves still clung to the gray twigs. "They have very few winter leaves. In summer, they smell sour. We rub the leaves on our skins, and the smell keeps away the shuteyes." She pictured for Leah a pesky flying insect similar to a gnat.

They stopped in the late afternoon at Ryl's farm, the place where Valad had captured Leah. Everything appeared to have returned to normal there, although an air of anxiety and recent shock hung over the place. Leah spotted half a dozen faces peering from windows and around corners as they rode into the yard. She wondered if Angin were there.

Thiele was suppressing agitation. Leah thought she was not entirely comfortable revealing to Matvar her connections to the farm. She could feel Matvar's interest, his not yet relinquished sense of duty. He still considered changing his mind, considered it and then remembered it was too late. Leah felt his despair before he shut himself away again. She had time to understand that his sorrow was not so much for the loss of his command, his career—that had apparently caused him much bitterness recently—but something much older and deeper. A bereavement; he had lost someone of great importance to him. A wife, Leah guessed. No, that was wrong. She wasn't even sure these people had spouses, as she understood the concept. It seemed more likely— she wasn't sure why—that the lost one was a blood relative, perhaps a sister.

Matvar did not like being at the farmhouse. If he had arrived in his official capacity with two pairs of soldiers, he would have known just how to treat these people and how to expect them to treat him. Now he was nothing. An exile, an outlaw, a follower of a Learned One. He was beginning to learn how much he must give up to be twin to a Sky Dweller. It was uncomfortable. He was relieved when the farm people showed no inclination to have anything to do with him. Some of them spoke to Leah after Thiele had gone off with the proprietor. Then they left him and Leah alone in the big front room. He leaned against the cushions of the soft chair and pretended to sleep.

About half a kroon later, a young woman brought them some food. It was better than Matvar had had in days, and he ate hungrily. Leah ate only setony and kerm. She had a sudden flash of memory of some food from her home world—so vivid that Matvar could taste it. She looked up at him and said a word in her own language, an apology for the intrusion. Matvar was surprised. He began to realize how careful of him she was trying to be, how unnatural the twintouch still felt to her.

Thiele came in alone as they were finishing. "We will not be staying here tonight," she announced. "The proprietor has given us food and some warm things for Leah, but he cannot give us shelter tonight." She looked at Leah. "I am sorry," she added. "There is a problem. He can't use it, and he won't allow me to use it. Orders from home."

There was something she wanted to keep obscure from him, but Matvar took the image from Leah: a meaningless assemblage of wire, metal, and glass objects, like a sacred relic. What use would such a thing have? Unless these people profaned such things by using them as ordinary wands. He did not think that was what Thiele meant. Leah was very disappointed.

"Is Angin here?" she asked. "Is she safe?"

"She is not here," said Thiele, "but as far as anyone knows, she is safe. You may see her again." She did not elaborate.

They took to the trail again and rode two kroons before Thiele led them aside to a camping spot she obviously knew well. No dreams of Rudvar haunted Matvar that night.

Six more days they traveled north. The forest changed. It was no longer a regrowth blotting out abandoned farmlands but—Leah surmised—the original virgin forest. Lofty hightower trees loomed over them sometimes or marched away over the hills, showing the path of their seeding vectors. There were mature blackwood trees also, saved from logging by their distance from populated lands.

Leah had once spent part of an autumn in New Hampshire. The colors had exploded out of summer almost overnight, only to be gone within two weeks. Here on Autumn, it was early October all the time. Her eyes began to hunger for green.

The land was not completely empty of people. Several times a day, for the first three days, Leah saw dwellings, including a few prosperous-looking farms like Ryl's. They stopped at two of these, although they did not remain long at either one. In each case, Thiele had some acquaintance with the proprietor, but there was no sign or mention of a radio. The travelers were always fed and sent on their way with a fresh supply of food.

After noon on the fourth day, there were no more farms. The wildness of the land was unbroken and the forest thinned out to grassland dotted with trees. Matvar began to break his silence more often that day. His spirits seemed to improve as the distance increased between him and the arena of his former duties. His behavior took on a courtliness, especially marked toward Thiele, but he was also courteous to Leah and spoke to her directly several times. She was aware he was trying to put their relationship on a more natural footing. He was not a man to whom this came easily, and she was touched he would make the effort. She responded with as much warmth as she thought he could accept.

About an hour after their midday rest the next day, the riders came upon a large herd of animals blocking the road. They were a startling orange shading to blue on legs and head, and in form something like a cross between a moose and a rhinoceros, with three palmate horns on head and snout. Thiele, who was riding in the lead, stopped a good hundred meters short of the milling bodies.

"Bosorn!" said Matvar. *Good hunting,* pronounced his regretful emanations.

"We'll have to get them to move," said Thiele with exasperation.

Matvar pulled his whip out of his belt. "Better to go around," he advised.

Thiele pointed her fingers downward in a gesture of dissent. "It is too marshy here. An ornit would have no trouble, but the kurvals would be bogged."

"Are they dangerous?" Leah whispered. No one answered. It was unnecessary. The beasts were dangerous, especially in such numbers, especially in stampede.

Thiele raised one hand. "Think of shuteyes," she instructed them silently.

Obediently, Leah concentrated on every annoying biting insect she could remember: gnats, mosquitoes, bushflies, deer flies. Yes, especially deer flies. The skin on the back of her neck prickled and itched. The bosorn began to swish their tails and flick their ears. Their feet stamped and shuffled. A few of them tossed their heads and snorted. One or two ambled off the road into the tall clumps of goldenlace, brushing their hides against the withered branches of curledge. A few more followed, and soon the whole mass were on the move, away from the road and the riders.

"Very nice!" said Leah. "Does it work on the insects, too?"

"Unfortunately not," Thiele replied.

THE HELL MACHINE

Valad grumbled to himself from the back of his mount as he rode north on the road with twenty retainers. That fungus-footed clod of a scout had sworn to him that Thiele, Matvar, the throwback, and their companions had fled this way, yet they had been riding for several kroons with no sign. Impossible, he thought to himself. She could not have been here, yet where else was he to look? Even if Matvar had taken her to Oshune, as he half-suspected, he was far out of reach in the opposite direction by now. He could only trust his scout was right, and Matvar had taken her north instead. His only other hope was Thiele might escape Matvar's clutches and return to him. He couldn't imagine Thiele leaving of her own free will, unless, perhaps, this was the final prank, the ultimate test of his affection. In that case, he did not intend to fail the challenge.

A roaring sound from the south caused the mounts to be edgy. Valad turned in that direction to see a green shape move toward them. It made a sound like distant thunder. Now it turned a bend in the road and came toward them, mowing down the brush at the side of the road as it came. Someone had revived a hell-machine from the dark times, no doubt. The kurvals of his escort screamed and bolted into the forest. Valad mastered his kurval as he sat, alone. The hell-machine ground to a stop in front of him.

Two throwbacks stood from the seats, shouting in an unknown tongue, and five big bugs were with them. Valad tried to thrust his irritation into their minds, but they did not flinch. Indeed, there was no mental murmuring coming from their direction at all. Were they mind-blind as well as mutant?

Valad brandished his whip at them. "I am an officer of the Twin Crowns. Get that hell-machine out of here, or I'll have your misbegotten heads!"

In answer, the ones in front waved to one side. He looked in that direction but saw nothing but forest.

He turned back to them, repeating his threat. He urged his mount forward slowly. In answer, they sat and started up the machine again. This time, he barely managed to control the kurval well enough to guide it to the side of the road as it tried to bolt. The machine rumbled by, blowing dust and plant bits into his face as it passed. Someone would pay for this. If not Matvar, if not the throwbacks, however many of them there were, then at least that hammer-toed scout who brought him in this direction.

FINDING TWINS

That evening, a low pall of clouds poured down from the northeast. It began to rain before dawn, lightly and steadily, the kind of rain that might linger for days; and continue it did, all that day and all night and into the morning as they climbed out of the grasslands into higher, more wooded country. Matvar reverted to sullen silence. Even Thiele seemed dispirited, although she told them they were getting near the end of the journey. Leah had to stop thinking about hot showers and low gravity; she was too miserable. You might think they'd be looking for her by now. Maybe they'd given her up. She'd be impossible to find in this wilderness. She should have made Thiele take her back to the wreck.

The sun came back at last one morning. Day dawned visibly, and when the sunlight reached them it was wonderfully warm. Steam rose from their wet clothing and the hides of the kurvals. A chorus of chipits arose from the matted rhizo along the road.

As the ground dried, they made better speed, even where they had to leave the old roadway to take the hidden, narrow trails that went past blockades of fallen rocks or trees. Thiele stoically accepted the need to let Matvar learn the secret way home.

As a token of return, Matvar kept watch for slaens while they were on the trails, but it was hardly necessary. The predators feared people and avoided roads. A hungry slaen might risk an ambush on a narrow wood-trail, but even that was unlikely.

At the end of the first detour on the next day, his vigilance was rewarded. He called a halt as they came out onto the roadway again and pointed at the rocks they had by-passed. "If that's your watchman, he's sleeping on duty," he commented.

"Watchman?" said Thiele. Beast halted, and she and Leah looked back, shading their eyes. "Palmo!" Thiele tumbled off Beast and scrambled in among the boulders.

"Hey!" said Leah. Her kurval was grunting and humping its back in response to the distress Thiele emitted. Matvar helped her down. Leah was slightly surprised—he usually avoided touching her. When he had convinced the kurvals they should stay put and spend some time grazing, he and Leah followed after Thiele.

She was weeping over the body on the rocks.

The man's eyes opened. He looked at them blurrily and groaned. There was a red weal across his face, just missing his eyes. "Um," he said.

"Koriam!" said Thiele. "What happened? What are you doing here? Where's Palmo?"

He tried to speak, but he was too hoarse.

Thiele fetched her water bottle and gave him a drink.

When his throat cleared, he said, "I wanted...." He stopped and looked around. "I don't remember. Who are these strangers?"

"Long story," Thiele said. "We'd better get you home first."

"Not till my head stops ringing," he said petulantly. "What've you been up to?"

Thiele explained as briefly as she could why she had brought Leah and Matvar with her.

"*That's* a Starborn?" said Koriam.

"Yes," said Leah, "but I'm not—"

"A Starborn!" said Koriam. "Well, then I suppose Palmo was right. We should call—Palmo!"

"What's wrong?" said Thiele, in alarm.

"You—Matvar—help me sit up." He groaned again as Matvar propped him up, then closed his eyes tight shut and concentrated on calling out mentally. He could not find any sign of his brother's existence.

Thiele took his hand, trying to join him in the sending.

Matvar stared at them in horror and reached out to feel Leah's presence. "His twin?" he asked in a whisper.

Twin? Leah repeated to herself. For the first time Matvar had "thought" to her directly. The underlying image was "he who shares the mind." Like us, Leah marveled. There was no reply.

Suddenly they felt Koriam's fear dissolve. Palmo was answering. It took him some moments to come awake enough to hear what Koriam "said."

Koriam repeated Thiele's story. "Get someone out here with a spare mount," he finished. "And tell Verret to put the sound-senders back on."

Palmo said something.

"Well, do the best you can." Koriam opened his eyes. "He doesn't think they'll take his word for it about sending sounds. It'll probably have to wait until we show up." He shifted and caught his breath. "Oh, gods, I hurt all over."

"What did happen?" said Matvar.

"I think Palmo got a whipping while we were linked. Help me up. I need to piss."

Matvar obliged again.

"Do you think you can ride?" asked Thiele when he was done.

"I suppose I'd better try."

Matvar tucked his whip away and lifted Koriam to the back of his kurval. She was beginning to realize it had been a mistake to get off her kurval. Wanting to be of some help, anyway, she began to gather up some pamphlets and sheets of paper that lay scattered where Koriam had lain. The writing was indecipherable, of course.

Writing! She held in her hands the first written material of this planet that anyone from her civilization had laid eyes on. Reverently, she brushed dirt off the pages. She caught a glimpse of a diagram in one. It reminded her of a horoscope or alchemical chart. What a lot there was to learn on this world! Why were they still wasting time on the moon?

She would have liked to examine her find more closely, but suddenly she felt herself under anguished scrutiny. She looked up to find Koriam staring at the papers in her hands. He tried to dismount, but Matvar and the kurval both protested against the imprudence.

"Did it rain last night?" said Koriam, trying to sound calm.

"No," said Thiele.

"Thank the gods!" he said, and having said it, looked doubtfully at Leah.

Matvar took the bridle and marched off, leading Koriam.

Thiele found the case for the papers and put them back into it. She helped Leah mount, and they set off after the men. Thiele pulled ahead and tried to force herself to rein back. It was difficult. She wanted to find out how Palmo was. She wanted to get to Palmo. She wanted....

"Ride ahead," Koriam suggested.

She hesitated, worrying about all three of her companions—Koriam for his injuries, Leah for her physical weakness, Matvar for his dependence on Leah. She looked anxiously at Matvar. He looked back, considering her. "Go ahead," he said quietly.

"Yes, all right," she said.

Beast gave a snort and took off. If there was Palmo at the end of the road, there was also a comfortable stable. In a few moments, they were out of sight.

Around mid-day, Verret reached them, riding one kurval and leading a spare.

"What the devils possessed you to go downhill?" she demanded of Koriam. "We've had searchers going up around your normal haunts all night."

"I'm sorry."

Verret stared at Leah. Skin without blue in it looked odd, and so did the curves of the breast, but deformities can be found in any population. "That romance Palmo spun wasn't true, was it?"

"Starborn, yes. Gods, no," said Leah.

"But...." Verret thought a moment. "Well, let's get you in. The sound-senders can wait till then."

"I forgot to ask for medicine," said Koriam abruptly.

"We managed to work that out ourselves," Verret said. She took out a flask with a syrup to deaden pain. "Not a full dose I'm afraid. You still have to ride."

"Ugh," said Koriam, at the taste.

"Here." She gave him some water.

When they came in sight of the main hall, Thiele was waiting cheerfully for them at the door and Angin and Kron with her. Leah waved at them.

"Palmo isn't so badly hurt, then," said Koriam, when he caught sight of Thiele.

"Need and ingenuity are twins," said Verret, quoting the proverb.

Leah felt depressed moving into a community of yet more strangers. They all knew where they belonged and what to do, but there was nothing for her. Then it occurred to her that she *didn't* feel like that. *She* was happy at the prospect of radio contact with home. Impatience for an answer and physical discomfort were not serious discouragements.

The kurvals halted. Matvar ignored Koriam and came to Leah's side to help her down. He looked up at her, blinking in the sunlight. His skin shone almost sky-blue in the brightness. "The gods return," he said, aloud and clearly-imaged in Leah's mind. "And I am a god's twin."

Before Leah could protest, a wonder froze them all to silence, goggling backward as a heap of metal came out of the woods nearby, following a creekbed. It was mounted on chains that crawled along like ennit grubs, at a speed more suited to a hungry slaen as it came rumbling up behind them.

The kurvals screeched and bolted for the stables. Leah and Koriam both fell, but Matvar on the one side, and Verret and Thiele on the other, caught them safely.

"Guards!" Verret called, mentally.

The metal hillock stopped, shuddered and fell silent. There were oddly shaped beings in it. A door opened in its side, and a person leaned out, carefully displaying open hands, empty of weapons.

"Hi," said !!!.

LEAH'S RIDE

!!! clambered out of the groundcar, supporting herself with her larger arms. (Leah sent the three clicks of !!!'s name telepathically to Matvar and the others. The Autumn Worlders puzzled over the name; Leah mentally explained they were supposed to be different clicks, but few non-Jheehan could make the distinctions acceptably.) She was followed by a five-group of Querlitzen and Leah's boss, Fragrant Melody of Bells. His skin glittered in the sunlight.

!!! shook herself to loosen fur matted from sitting too long and patted Leah's head in greeting. "So you're here. We thought following that burst of radio activity might get us somewhere, but we weren't sure." She looked carefully at the Autumn Worlders around them, apparently suspecting them of preventing Leah from sending a proper distress signal.

Leah started to say it must have been one of Thiele's people who had tried to broadcast, but a Querlitzen with turquoise stones interrupted. "Are you the only survivor?"

"I don't think so. I hope Topaz and Diamond are all right, but I've lost them."

The Jheehan tsked and the Hultzu gave a whistle at the confirmation of their fears. Failure to locate their fellows telepathically had made death seem likely, especially where a Jheehan was concerned.

The Querlitzen consulted telepathically among themselves.

"I'm sorry I couldn't leave a clearer trail, said Leah. "It took you a long time to find me."

!!! said nothing.

Melody flushed green.

"No!" said Leah, suspicion dawning. "You don't mean Station-commander wouldn't let you come?" But she could see they did.

It had not taken them long to find her—it had taken them a long time to get permission to come looking. The Hultzu belief in the uniqueness of species was obviously accurate and usually harmless. Different species were different. Hultzu and Earthers looked a good deal alike, but a blush revealed the difference between copper-based and iron-based bloods. Some Hultzu had felt affronted at meeting so Hultzoid a species, until they learned the Earthers were not telepathic. The Hultzu were still unique—which was the point that mattered to some. Now here were these Hultzoid-looking Autumn Worlders. But had Station-commander known what they looked like? If she'd sent down a probe on a lander—and kept it secret—she might. Natives who looked like Hultzu or like Earthers, and who were either telepathic, like Hultzu, or not, like Earthers. Leah began to guess why their Station-commander, a Hultzu, had delayed direct exploration of the planet, overruling Fragrant Melody of Bells's recommendations.

"I did not know," said Melody, who sighed tunefully and added, "I should have guessed from so much privacy of meditations."

Leah wondered vaguely who had figured out the station commander's mania, and might have asked, but was distracted by suddenly recognizing a further implication of the betrayal. "That explosion Topaz and Diamond remembered—Station-commander wouldn't've deliberately—"

"Station-commander would," said !!!. "Your ship was sabotaged."

Melody turned greener still.

Verret meanwhile had overcome her astonishment and took charge. She firmly ordered everyone into the meeting hall to be fed and to give an account of themselves. Many of the community who could leave their work just then left it and crowded in with them to listen.

Baths and beds would have been more welcome to the travelers, but the force of curiosity was too strong.

Melody wanted to take advantage of the audience to deliver an explanatory speech on the Spiral Cooperative, but telepathy was not usually effective between species. He could not make himself understood by the Autumn Worlders. Leah offered to translate, but felt unsure of her ability to come up with equivalents for the more complicated terms. Melody decided to wait until he could speak for himself. His voice had the range and richness his people prized, and he did not like to depend on the harsher tones of an Earther's throat.

Thiele, joined by Angin and Kron, told the Learned Ones their adventures on the road. (They'd heard Angin and Kron before, but not, said Verret dryly, with full appreciation of the context.) Matvar was asked, but he said if he didn't have to he didn't want to, and they did not press him. Behind Thiele, the spaceport mural sent its fresco ships soaring the full length of the wall.

The party from the moon-station understood little of it, but taped it all and toyed with their food.

Leah gobbled down the things she knew she could eat safely. Some of the vegetables were fresh, raised under glass, she decided after puzzling the matter out.

A healer tried to get Koriam to leave and have his injuries seen to, but he was too fascinated and kept going on another dose of pain-killer and cups of sourstrap tea, heavily sweetened.

A man with a baby on his back came in while Thiele was talking, and Leah could feel them lighting up with joy at this reunion. She looked from Koriam to the newcomer with some surprise, chewing her bread more slowly.

Koriam looked at her, surprised by her surprise. "Why should Drummos look like me?"

"Who?" said Leah.

"Oh!" He laughed, and stopped, finding it painful. "That's not my brother. The healers are threatening to chain Palmo up if he exerts himself any more."

"Good idea, except maybe we should try it on you," murmured the healer who was keeping an eye on Koriam.

"Being a Head has advantages," said Koriam. "I stay."

The healer spread his hands resignedly.

Thiele finished her account and ran to embrace the stranger while Angin took up the tale.

Koriam turned again to Leah. "Drummos is Thiele's twin."

For a moment Leah was even more baffled, knowing too much through both Matvar and Koriam of the Blessing of an identical twin. Then she remembered that twins can be fraternal.

A woman with a child on her back had joined the brother and sister—Drummos's mate with their other child, Leah guessed.

"Good for those youngsters to have their twin-mother around for a while," Verret said to Koriam. "Do you think Palmo and Drummos can persuade her to stick around a few seasons, or do we need her more on the road?"

"Hard to say," Koriam replied. "Might's well leave it alone."

Verret frowned.

Angin came to an end, leaving Thiele looking startled as she realized that Akashtai's name of Jumper-friend was after all not a dream, but truth. Angin gave her a grin, then sat down and looked at Leah.

Kron looked sideways at Angin. "I'll have to be getting back to Ryl soon. Will you want to go home then, too?"

"I'm not sure. I think Akashtai would like me to travel for a while, away from…I need to learn my own dances to add to hers."

"Could she learn to be one of our scouts?" Thiele asked Verret and Koriam.

"Umm," said Verret, and asked Angin, "Would you wish it?"

"Yes. I think I would."

"I'll tell Ryl to expect his ornit back later, then," said Kron. "That one's hard to lead."

"What about the Starborn's account?" said Verret.

"Me?" said Leah.

Melody said, "You have told these people too much already. Say no more."

Verret, picking up the sense of this, snapped, "Tell your lord we are neither fools nor children to be sheltered from truth."

Melody stuck out his elbows. "They are as children to us in knowledge—"

"I don't think that's exactly correct," Leah said. She nodded at the spaceport mural.

Melody hummed a phrase and smoothed one hand along an imaginary incline. After a moment, he said, "If you will permit us to send an observer among you, we will know better after a year or so how much your peoples can absorb." Leah translated this.

Verret and Koriam exchanged a look. Verret said, "We will hear what the scholar Leah has to say for herself, or we will give no such permission. That's a fair price—more than fair."

It would have been impractical to claim that their observer could go elsewhere on the planet where the Learned Ones would not hear of it—not with wanderers like Thiele as a substantial portion of the group. "Go ahead," he told Leah.

Telepaths, Leah decided, made the prospect of public speaking even more daunting than it was by its nature. Thiele's people were keenly attentive. Matvar was too gloomy to be paying attention, but she could not help feeling his gloom. She could not feel the feelings of the others directly, but it seemed to her that she understood them a little more than she would have expected to do simply from visual signs. Melody, although carefully relaxed in his chair, was envious of her for having made the First Contact and angry over the irregularities of the situation. The five Querlitzen were presumably trying to call Topaz and Diamond. She could not sense the calls, but a mood of anxiety jittered over the five. !!! was pleased to have found her, sad that others had died. With one mood and another, it was all very distracting.

How do you concentrate? she asked Matvar.

He focused on the mural, grunted, and fell telepathically silent. She tried focusing on a hot-house bouquet of red flares on the table, the peppery-sweet smell of their spikes, the helixes formed by the long yellow leaves coming up from the orange stems. It helped. The other emotions faded, leaving only a buzz on top of the normal stage fright. She took a gulp of water, and began her own account, speaking alternately in Standard and her new tongue.

She had to give up her mental isolation within a few sentences to get help with vocabulary and phrasing, but at least she'd had a chance to catch her breath.

The news that the Autumn Worlders could read Leah's mind startled the group from the Station. They were all used to the Earther handicap of non-telepathy. Melody caught his breath, seemed to hesitate a moment between a laugh and a curse, and shaded his face with his hand. Leah could not tell what expression dominated in the shadow. !!! fidgeted, clasping and unclasping her smaller hands.

Leah was interrupted again. The five Querlitzen, although they did not move a muscle, seemed as if they were running in circles in a victory dance with mandibles clicking and antennae quivering: Topaz and Diamond had answered. They were alive nearby and would find their way out of the forest to join them shortly.

"Thank Peace!" Leah said, and Melody let his hand drop back to his side.

Leah drank more water and went on. When she came to the Jumpers, she found she had to be brief because the illusions they wove made it hard to remember or describe them, but even so, both Melody and the Learned Ones realized this was an unknown and important people who should be sought out—assuming they could be convinced to agree to the intrusion. Near the end, she noticed with amusement that Melody went rigid in his chair when she described Koriam's stack of papers, and that Koriam and Verret were exchanging another look at his reaction. Another good bargaining point. The Brokers took note.

Something was still bothering the Querlitzen, but she could not make out what it was.

She gave up on the last couple of sentences entirely and stood tiptoe, craning her neck for a better look out the door as a clatter of several Querlitzen feet became audible.

Topaz and Diamond trotted in.

A child—the one who had helped attack her—was riding on Topaz. He was sucking his fingers again.

The three-fold unit—Topaz, Diamond, and child—said in unison and two languages, "Here I am!"

Leah, Melody, and !!! all said, "That's impossible!"

The five-fold Querlitzen said in horrified unison, "That's obscene."

The child fell off Topaz and burst into tears of grief and rage as his union with Topaz and Diamond broke.

Drummos left his own child with her mother and twin and went to pick the youngster up and cuddle him, but the tot was inconsolable.

"What is going on?" demanded a Querlitzen with jade inlay, but Topaz and Diamond as a two-fold suffering again the loss of a part of their unity could not say much more than, "We follow, we are here."

The boy wailed, louder and louder. The howling reminded Leah of the single-minded intensity of a beagle.

In the south, thought Matvar, *we have a breed of tame fossa we use for hunting, but they only bark. Do your hunt animals truly make a noise like this?*

The beagles do, thought Leah.

The turquoised Querlitzen said, "Can't anyone stop that noise?"

The child wriggled out of Drummos's arms and scrambled up on Diamond's back, where he clung in silence.

The three-fold union explained, in alternate languages, "I was hungry, for I could not find things to eat/I was hungry, for the lord's men turned us out in the wilderness in winter/I met/I thought there would be food further away, where there were not so many people searching for the spring-fruits/I had to follow you/I followed you far away."

"Where are your parents?" said Thiele, and

"Where is your twin?" said Matvar.

"Here," the three-fold union said, either ignoring the first question or taking both questions as a request for the identity of nearest-kin.

Thiele tried again. "What is your name?"

"Topaz/Diamond/Topaz-Diamond."

"Obscene!" the five-fold Querlitzen said again, but the three-fold union was not so easily shaken by the blast of disapproval now, and the child stayed where he was.

The five-fold Querlitzen shuddered, then made the effort and addressed the three-fold union, "You are not whole now. You will see more clearly when you are whole—but you must see even now that this will not do. You cannot grow up in such disparate segments."

It was not clear if this was a euphemism for telling Topaz and Diamond that having sex with an Autumn Worlder riding along would be difficult, or if they were actually speaking to the child and asserting his need for others of his kind, or both.

The threesome conferred within itself, and the others could not pick up what they said.

Leah could not help thinking that the experiment of continuing the unity might be of use to the Querlitzen—it might be good for them to have the option of closer contact with those different from themselves. But running the experiment on a child was open to ethical objection, and it rather looked as if only an Autumn child had the malleability to enter into it.

What considerations swayed them they could never explain afterwards. Topaz and Diamond alone lacked the intelligence to understand or remember, and the child lacked the maturity.

The youngster slid off Diamond's back, took a step, stumbled, gave up on two-legged, grown-up locomotion as too upsetting, and crawled over to Drummos.

"What's your name?" said Drummos.

"I forget."

"Listen," Thiele said, and stooped beside him. "Your kinfolk took Leah's metal-band. They must have traded it for food. They could be all right. We could take you home."

"No!" said the child. "Starve *next* winter."

Thiele looked at him and at Drummos, and turned to Koriam and Verret. "I'm afraid he's right," she said in a low voice. "That's Valad's territory, and a bad place to be while he stays in power."

"If we can find I-Forget's kin," said Koriam, "we might be able to help them settle somewhere in the north."

"I wouldn't trust them that close. They've learned banditry, and it's a hard lesson to unlearn. Maybe we could help them go somewhere else—but they may have fled already. For that matter, Valad is fairly careful about his duties as a magistrate—he may have caught them for theft and executed them."

"We'll try anyway," said Verret, "but we'll keep in mind the likelihood of not being able to send him back."

"First pairs first," said Drummos. "Food and drink." He coaxed the boy over to the long table and got him to take his fingers out of his mouth and start putting kerm-muffins with skerry jam in.

The seven-fold Querlitzen were closed in on themselves in a private debate that seemed nowhere near resolution.

Koriam turned his attention to Matvar. "Have you thought what you may wish to do among us?"

"I've thought, but found no answers. I am trained as an officer of the guard. You can't use me as a guard until you feel sure you can trust me."

"I trust your word," said Thiele, "and I'm considered a good judge."

"Will you give your word?" said Koriam. "Though if you want to go back, perhaps we could work something out—erasing some memories, perhaps, if you agree—"

"—experts might be able to restore them. But with the Veen holding more power now, I'd get into trouble no matter what happened, I think." He looked directly at Leah for the first time since she began her speech. "The gods say they're not gods. I'm a religious man, and I don't know what that can mean, but I'd rather try to find out than never hope to know. Here's the best place to try." He thought, *You could be your people's observer here. You could stay.*

Leah thought, *No, I can't. Melody wants it, and he's head of the department. I can't stop him from taking over here. Though Justice knows if he tries to get his name first on the byline when we do a report, I'll skin him and recycle the hide. But for the full-time observational post—I can't manage your gravity. Hultzus are used to this kind of weight.*

You managed it well enough, thought Matvar.

For a little while. He'll need help sometimes. I'll be visiting.

How often? How long?

I don't know.

Matvar said, "I give my word."

There was a moment of silence, except for the sounds of people clearing away their dishes.

Melody said, "I think this is a time of farewells." He hesitated and added, "If you will permit it, I will stay behind and begin my time of observation directly."

The Brokers had been waiting for their next bargaining point to come up. "Granted," said Koriam, "if I go in your place as our observer among your people."

"Certainly not!" said the Hultzu.

"Let me go!" said Matvar simultaneously. He thought, *You must agree. It's obviously the best plan.*

Leah thought, *Is it? Koriam is better trained for that kind of work.*

Matvar thought, *Is that all? I could be trained.*

Leah thought, *Not quickly.*

"He's ill," Matvar said aloud. "And he doesn't know what it's like to go out of twin-touch. He'll never stand it."

"You did," said Koriam. "I may even heal faster out of touch with Palmo's injuries—"

The healer who had been watching him looked doubtful, but after a moment's thought hesitantly waved agreement.

—and there's the sound-sender. I can call and—" He broke off, and grinned ruefully. "Verret, maybe you'd better do it. I don't know if I can bear to go away until I know if my silicon flakes work."

"That's tempting," Verret said, "but I think I'm better at the detail work here than you are, so it'll be easier for us to spare you. Or we could be generous and let another scholar volunteer for it, but you'd be our best choice for studying their machinery, and—"

Koriam suddenly realized that this logical answer was going on too long, and he was being teased. "What? What happened?"

"They were tested last night. They work."

Koriam gave a hoot of triumph, cutting it short only in deference to his bruises.

Melody, meanwhile, was watching them with a mixture of doubt and respect. "I did say no," he said.

"So you did," said Verret. "Do you want to hold to it and wait for us to decide when it's convenient to let you come back?"

Fragrant Melody of Bells rose gracefully from his chair and glowered down. "I stay," he said at last.

And I stay, Matvar thought regretfully. *I lived through it once. If you bring so much singleness into the world, maybe you are truly not the gods.*

I keep telling you that, Leah thought.

Matvar thought, *If I have to think impossible thoughts, I suppose I have come to the right place. The Learned Ones are famous for it—but I never thought to be Learned.*

She hugged him, and his back stiffened against this undignified behavior. Then he tried to relax. A twin on his dignity with his twin? He accepted her embrace, and they shared their mixed feelings, finding doubts and hopes inseparable. Besides worrying over his own loss when distance broke the twin touch and left them alone again, Matvar worried over Leah. She tried to assure him that she would be all right—it was something she had known so short a time it would not be difficult to go without a twin again—but then she realized that she was not sure that it was so. She fell back on the hope Koriam had suggested for Matvar: *It can be done. You did it. There'll be visits.*

If you could replace your lord here, one day—or if I could replace Koriam....

Ifs seemed to multiply around them. Leah felt dizzied with them.

Matvar let her go, waiting for her to recover balance.

Thiele and Angin came to embrace her, and the time of farewells threatened to extend indefinitely.

Gently, Fragrant Melody of Bells shooed Leah away and out the door. He helped her get into the groundcar, then Koriam, !!!, and the seven Querlitzen. He glided back.

!!! started the car, and they roared away into the shadow of the trees, on their way to the ship, and the Moon.

EPILOGUE

Peridot's exoskeleton, dried and cleaned, was taken indoors at last. The aristocrat who rode out of the inn to search for his freakish prisoner had not returned. The innkeeper did not much care. He knew a bait for trade when he saw one.

A Wonder from the Skies, he billed it, and the customers who came to gawk at the jeweled armor that had fallen from the stars in flame had themselves a good time arguing over whether such jewels were what made the smallest moon shine, or, in vast quantities, caused the brightness of the sun, or whether the Starborn had sent them a sign of their imminent return or a gracious mark of their approval, flung from the furthest heavens, of the new queens of the Twin Crowns. The gold-green jewels flashed by candlelight.

The innkeeper served good food and good drinks and offered no opinion. A Wonder from the Skies, he said, was enough for him to know.

APPENDIX:
SOME FAUNA AND FLORA OF AUTUMN WORLD

Note: The following are local names and descriptions given to Leah by the local people she met, with additions given later to Fragrant Melody of Bells. As yet there are no offworld names or classifications.

ANIMALS, WILD

BOSORN

Large wild herbivore. Buffalo sized. Deep orange hide, shading to blue on legs and head. Three horns on nose and forehead, spreading into large palms six to eight inches wide, ten to twelve inches long. Found in large herds on the plains country below the woodlands that stretch south and west of the Angin River country. In smaller herds of 10-48 they also travel much farther north, along the rivers and streams and the grassy rides formed by old roads, and through open woodland. Hunted by the gentry for meat, horns, and hides. Sometimes killed by the peasantry, too, when they move into cultivated areas, but since these animals are dangerous, peasants hunt them only when it's necessary, and not for sport.

DROMIL

Thick-bodied, long-haired animal of the flats and woodlands of the far northern peninsulas and coasts. Muskox sized. Two long, coiled, forward-projecting horns. Their thick hair is maroon to purple, with a curly purple-brown undercoat. Their diet, winter and summer, is mostly rhizo, with some leaves of shrubs and low-growing trees. In winter they migrate south some distance into thicker forests. Their broad, padded feet make it possible for them to occupy boggy and marshy areas. They travel in small herds of 5-15; one leading male, with females and younger males, young in season. In summer, the curly undercoat is shed; people in the north collect this, spin it, and weave a good quality warm cloth. The Brokers of Knowledge sometimes kill them for food or their thick hides.

LOPER

These are slender-bodied, long-legged wild herbivores, grass eaters like the bosorns. There are two varieties: plains and forest. The plains Loper can be found in the same territory as the Bosorn, in loosely spread out herds of anywhere from 10-25 or so. Forest Lopers are solitary except at mating time; the young leave their mothers at about eight months.

The plains Loper is larger (deer sized), dappled orange and light brown in color, with two horns projecting out on each side of the forehead, forked at the tip. Forest Lopers are smaller (goat sized), dappled in darker shades, sometimes almost a dark red. They have two short, forward-projecting horns, with no fork at the tip. Both types are long boned with three long toes on each foot, giving them a springy, leaping gait.

WATERSLIDER

A gray or brown, sleek-furred mammal, half the size of an otter. The four legs are flattened almost like fins, and flaps of fur-covered skin extend between the legs on each side for swimming and floating. Has claws for burrowing. Lives in burrows in stream banks, but spends much of its time in the water, catching fish (the local equivalent), water insects, etc. This animal hibernates for 6-8 weeks in the depth of winter; it will break ice to get at creatures underneath for food at other times during the winter.

FOSSA

Fox-sized predator with a doglike head and clawed feet. Runs like a fox, but can also climb trees; its legs and claws are partly adapted to this. Woodland fossa has orange and yellow stripes; northern fossa is larger, striped maroon and gray. It is a scavenger and an omnivore. Preys on small mammals, insects, birds, and eggs, also root vegetables, fruits, any kind of offal, etc. Can be a pest in cultivated areas, but also serves to control chumpers and mineks. If caught young, fossas can be tamed.

SLAEN

Large, powerful predator. Leopard sized. Long stabbing incisors, long head with heavy jaws and curved, retractable claws. Fast runner. Forest and plains-living slaens have yellow-orange-red mottled hide that gives good camouflage. Snowslaens, in the far north, have similar coats but in darker shades. In winter, they develop patches of white. Generally remain in deep forest, or heavy brush in plains areas. Prey on all the larger herbivores including the domestic varieties but generally avoid people unless they are very hungry. A solitary, wounded person can be in danger, however.

BINDIGID

A small, peccary-sized browsing animal found in forested areas. Occur in small family-sized herds of 5-8 individuals, although young males are solitaries. Have small clawed feet, long noses, short stiff hair that is dark red, with yellow to yellow-brown spots. Eat low-growing leaves, nuts, fungi, roots and grubs, digging up the earth with their claws and turning over clods, small logs, etc. Have thick, furry tails that they carry curled over their backs—

these are in some demand for ruffs on winter coats, gloves, and such. They make little bleating noises as they move through the forest, shrill whistles when disturbed. Alive, they have a somewhat rank smell, but they clean up nicely for cooking. A two-year-old male would make a meal for several people.

CHUMPER

Small burrowing animal. Hair is red, shading to orange. Lives all over the place. Eats seeds, grubs, insects, small fruit, roots. Not a climber, although its forepaws are so handlike that some of the people (not only peasants) are a bit superstitious about them—they once were people but were punished by Ashven for some terrible crime. However, this doesn't keep them from being killed when they become a pest in the cultivated parts, although they are *not* eaten, except by fossas.

MINEK

General name for several types of very small, burrowing or ground-nesting, rodentlike animals (small ones mouse sized, larger ones the size of small rabbits). Generally have long snouts, triangle-shaped ears, four clawed feet, no tail. Colors vary from yellow to brown to yellowish-brown or shades of orange. Eaters of most kinds of vegetable food including grain. Can be a severe problem in farms, villages, and other settled areas at harvest time.

SICKLEWING

A flying mammal. Smooth, sleek gray fur. About the size of a flying squirrel, but with long, sickle-curved wings. Builds nest in tall trees not far from water, and dives for fish and insect larvae.

ANIMALS, DOMESTIC

BROCKNEY

The general, all-purpose, domesticated animal. A large, thick-bodied animal, heavy legs, squareish head on thick curved neck. Single short thick horn on end on nose. Gray with wide stripes of gray-yellow. Heavy padded feet with four wide, short toes. Not used for riding, but pulls wagons, plows, any heavy load. Used for meat, milk, hides, and leather. Horns are used for drinking mugs, mounted in wood or metal bases. Bone and almost every other part is used for something. Its dung is the most important source of fertilizer. Eats any vegetation or roots, but does best on firn. No wild variation of species.

AMBLER

Small four-legged, long-haired animal, donkey-sized. Can be any color from cream to dark brown; has small horns behind ears. Slow but steady, used to pull carts or to carry loads, although it doesn't have the capacity of a brockney. The hair is woven into cloth, which may be left the natural color or dyed. Peasants also use these animals for riding; they are slow but will keep going for long periods. Raised throughout the continent. Diet same as Brockney. No wild variation of species.

ORNIT

A two-legged riding animal—a bit like a cross between an ostrich and a camel. Two powerful, muscular legs, feathery-looking brown hair, straight back. Broad splayed feet with thick webbing of furred skin lets it travel in boggy areas. Very hardy, adaptable to many climates; can live on almost any type of vegetation. Covers long distances at a steady pace, but its top speed can only be used for short sprints. Carries two people if each is not too heavy. This animal may have been introduced at the time of the old galactic settlement. Used mostly in forested areas.

KURVAL

Four-legged riding animal, larger than an ambler, strong and graceful. Size of a quarter horse. Piebald in many shades and combinations—brown and yellow, dark red and cream, orange and gray, etc. Ridden by the military and People Who Are Somebody. Wealthy people may use them to pull passenger carriages, chariots, and so on. Most common in the Oshune area, but among the Knowledge Brokers and their friends, they are bred for general use. Eats hay made from firn or kerm stalks and will browse on rhizo or other plants.

BIRDS, INLAND

JINGLER

Robin-sized yellow and white bird. Walks up and down the sides of trees, searching for the grubs under the bark. Call is a series of tones like a bell.

LERIOLE

Sparrow-sized bright red birds, eaters of flying insects. Cluster freely around human settlements and buildings, nesting on roofs, going for the insects stirred up by domestic animals, also taking some weed seeds. Call is a sharp whistle.

ORTALIN

A large, turkey-sized ground bird, but with larger wing span—unlike turkeys, they are good flyers. Bright yellow feathers barred in patterns of green, white, and blue. Female has brighter colors, more green, an orange crest. They travel in mated pairs, migrating to the far southern hemisphere in the winter. In spring, they return to the north; after mating, the male will brood the eggs. They nest in low trees or in dense shrubbery, in hedgerows, the forest edges, and open parts of the forest. They live largely on burrnuts and seeds from various trees. Call is a loud screech. These birds are hunted and make very good eating.

PERIT

A very small bird (wren sized) with blue-brown plumage. Nests chiefly in holes in plamon trees with their dark blue bark. Eats mostly insects and grubs. Call is a peep-peep-peep, repeated over and over.

RIVERHOVER

A large bird with wide, leathery-looking, kite shaped wings. Appears batlike, but is a true bird, not a flying mammal. Plumage is brown. Spends much time in flight over rivers, streams, and pools catching flying insects. Call is a high-pitched warble.

SAKERET

A large bird of prey, eagle-sized. Plumage is scarlet with a yellow breast. Attacks small mammals, young fossas, smaller birds. Call is a sweet, cooing warble. In spring they make their way north from wintering areas near Oshune and along the southern coasts.

SKYPOUNCER

A scavenger and eater of carrion. Will also attack young birds of other species in the nest. Vulture-sized, but wingspread is longer and shape is more slender. Plumage is mottled dark orange and blue. Appears V-shaped in flight. Prevalent throughout the northern half of the continent. Call is "Rawk! Rawk!"

WHEEDLER

A bird somewhat larger than a blackbird. Has barred plumage, black and purple. Eats seeds and scraps of bread, cereal, etc. Lives in northern woods, and in villages and on farmsteads. Call has a whistling, "wheedling" tone.

BIRDS OF THE SEACOAST

FARFARER

A very large bird (albatross-sized), dark blue on back and wings, white underneath. Spend most of their time out at sea. In spring, they come in to the northern coasts to nest, continuing to fly out to sea for food. Dives for fish. Call is a loud squawk.

GREEN DIVER

A bird of the coast, sometimes following the course of rivers inland for some distance. Dark green plumage. They hover above the water at its edge, diving for small fish, also take grubs and chrysalises of beach hoppers and such.

TERNILS

Another coastal bird, sandpiper sized, migrating north in spring and south to the end of the continent in autumn, but spending most of the time in between on the beaches and riverbanks. Plumage is deep red. They probe the sand and shallow water for shellfish, water bugs, etc. Call is "wheet, wheet, wheet."

A FEW OF THE MORE IMPORTANT INSECTS

The insects have not been closely investigated, but appear to have four legs and one-piece, flexible bodies in general.

CHIPITS

A small chirping insect, cricket-sized, found pretty well all over the continent. Pink or yellow with transparent wings. Not a pest. Preyed on by birds, chumpers, fossas, etc.

ENNIT

Small colonial insect, ant-sized. Red color. Builds donut-shaped mounds, 2-4 inches high and 12-24 inches around. Will sting if disturbed in their mounds but not generally a pest as the mounds tend to be built long distances apart.

HONEYSEEK

The major pollinating insect of the northern half of the continent. Wasp sized, ochre color. They build colonies underground. Most die off at the end of summer, a few remaining to live on stored food over the winter and start the colony off in the spring again.

INT

A pesky insect similar in size and habit to fleas. White color, including wings. May infest both wild and domestic animals; some varieties attack birds, and a few attack people. Can be a problem in stables especially.

LACEWINGS

General name for a family of insects ranging in size from $1/2$-4 inches in size, with wide lacy wings. Colors are varied. Eaten by many birds. Hatch out from eggs laid in water the previous autumn. (These are a source of food for fish and other water creatures.) In autumn, they begin to swarm for mating, and they become a pest for humans, forming great clouds around water sources, but in spring and summer they are harmless. Live throughout the continent.

SHUTEYE

A pesky flyer, similar to gnats, blackflies, etc. Tiny (gnat sized) and purple. The adults die off at the beginning of winter, and the new generation doesn't hatch out until early summer. They are a severe pest throughout the summer and fall.

TREES

The leaves of the trees on Autumn World range from pale yellow to deep orange or rust, bright scarlet to maroon, all year round; hence the name Earthers called the world. Most trees of Autumn World have scaly-appearing bark and grow two crops of leaves: smaller, darker, fleshier leaves in winter, often covered with a fine hair-like fuzz. These are shed in early spring and the lighter, larger leaves of summer appear. The following trees grow throughout the continent.

BIRKA

Slender supple trees with dark purple trunks and long trailing branches; winter leaves are tiny, dark red; summer leaves are yellow, long and narrow. Common along streams, in marshy areas, and all over the northern coastal flats. Grows 15-20 feet tall.

BHESHWOOD

Medium brown papery bark that tends to shed in strips as the tree grows; yellow winter leaves, scarlet summer leaves. After the winter leaves fall, and before the summer leaves show, they produce clusters of black flowers on long stems. These have a mild, soapy fragrance. Grows 30-50 feet tall.

BLACKWOOD

Handsome black-barked tree with dense wood that is black all the way through. One of the tallest trees. Spreading, regularly spaced branches. Winter leaves are few, small, maroon; they fall late in winter, well before the orange summer leaves begin to show and produce their spicy aroma. These trees with their fine-grained wood are prized for making furniture. Grows 70 feet tall.

CHATOLPA

Dark gray bark and wood. No winter leaves. In spring the branches are covered with orange, sweet-scented flowers; later there will be heart-shaped, yellow-orange leaves. Grows 60-65 feet tall.

DARKLEAF

Gray-red bark, light gray wood veined with maroon. Winter leaves are purple. Summer leaves come early; they are small, circular, and borne in a single clump of small branches at the tip of the trunk. These leaves are maroon in color. The leaf colors give the darkleaf its name. This tree is common along rivers and streams and in marshy or low-lying areas. Grows l8-20 feet tall.

HIGHTOWER

The tallest tree of the central and northern forests. Gray bark and nearly white wood, massive trunks. Winter leaves are deep orange. Lacy yellow summer foliage begins to appear before the winter leaves are completely shed. Branches start high on the trunks, and form high, spherical crowns. Grows 90-l00 feet tall.

PLAMON

Small slender trees with dark blue bark, upward-reaching branches. Red-purple winter leaves fall early; summer leaves are diamond-shaped, red. These trees often grow in small clumps of 5 or 6 under the shade of the hightowers, but also grow singly throughout the area. Grows 12-18 feet tall.

POMPONIA

Nearly white bark, deeply ridged instead of scaly. No winter leaves. Summer leaves come late in spring, are bright yellow with five or six lobes. Grows 50-60 feet tall.

RESIN TREES

Gray-brown bark. Thick, fleshy, "needle-like" bronze leaves growing in clusters all over the branches. These do not shed their leaves or grow winter leaves. Old leaves darken somewhat during the winter; the new year's growth is bright orange. This foliage has a resinous smell. There are several varieties differing in height and environment; some are found in lowland areas, others may grow in marshy areas or on hills and mountains. Grow 25-50 feet tall.

SKERRY

Gray-blue bark. These trees also have small fleshy leaves that never fall; they are bright yellow to rust in color, overlaid with a coat of gray hairlike fuzz in winter, much thicker than that found on some other trees, like the birka, darkleaf, or bheshwood. In spring this coating is shed. These trees produce a plumlike orange fruit in autumn; it is slightly tart, but makes excellent preserves and a ciderlike beverage. Grows 40-50 feet tall.

A SELECTION OF PLANT SPECIES

BLUE-EYE

A tiny wildflower that grows close to the ground. Fine yellow stems with short round leaves. Circle of oval petals may be any color from white to deep purple, but have centers of sky blue. Found in shady patches throughout the area.

CURLEDGE

Small gnarled shrubs that tend to grow along the open borders where the road passes through the trees. Also found in hedgerows. Gray bark; winter leaves are few, blue in color, ruffled edges. Yellow summer leaves, also ruffled, come late in spring. This plant has a slightly sour odor; summer leaves are used as insect repellent. Grows 4-5 feet tall.

FIRN

Refers to a variety of grass-like plants. These have clusters of tall, slender leaves growing from underground tubers. Colors are shades of yellow. They spread to cover any open, fairly dry ground. Dry and turn white in winter; new firn grows up in spring from the tubers. Height varies according to type. Plains, meadows, and "grassland" are covered with firn. The chief food of the large herbivores. Grows 6 inches-4 feet tall.

FLUFFHEAD

Low growing flowers with rosettes of yellow leaves, blue or green blossoms look much like a cotton ball. Grow in clumps and patches on open ground or meadows, or in open forest glades. Grows 10-15 inches tall.

GREYSTALK

A tall plant consisting mostly of clusters of stiff gray stems; long, thin orange leaves are almost hidden. The leaves are shed in autumn. In spring, new stems, yellowish at first, come up around the base of the existing clump. These lengthen, turn gray, and finally produce leaves. Found on thin, rocky soil or on barren ground. Grows 4-6 feet tall.

GOLDEN LACE

This plant forms a finely-interlocking network of springy, yellow stems with oval yellow leaves, giving a definite lacy look. In some places it forms great bands of color. In other areas it may grow as single shrubs or clusters of same. The far northern variety is a paler color. When pressed down, it will gradually spring back into shape again. Found along hillsides. Grows up to 3 feet tall.

KERM

The major food grain. Domesticated plant. The thick, many-branched stems are yellow-orange, with large ovate, rough leaves. The top of the stalk produces a cluster of finer stems that are covered with large seeds. These ripen to blue in autumn. The seeds are harvested and can be cooled like porridge or ground into flour. They contain a factor equivalent to gluten, and so will produce a raised bread. Raised in field. No wild species.

PLUMIOLE

These plants appear like feathers or large clusters of same. Yellow to yellow-orange in color; in summer they produce small, deep-orange flowers along the midribs. These are annual-perennial, the old plants dying away in the fall, new ones springing up, self-seeded in early spring. The dried fronds of autumn are collected and used for animal bedding (and sometimes for people, too), as they repel mineks. Freak types are reported from the deep forests. Can also be used as fodder for brockneys, amblers, and ornits. (Kurvals must have some type of firn.) Grows up to 6 feet tall.

RED EEL

A ground-covering vine. Southern and forest varieties have bright red stems, with small round leaves also red. Leaves have a pattern of veining that looks a bit like a small face. Northern varieties have paler stems with mottlings of blue or gray, and blue-purple leaves that look even more facelike. Grows 10-12 inches high; a spreading creeper.

RED FLARE

One of the earliest spring flowers. The plants tend to be spaced some distance apart, do not form clumps. Thick orange stems, arrow-shaped yellow leaves spiraling up around them, vivid scarlet blooms formed of many tiny florets, look from a distance like a flame. Found in open land around farms and villages. Grow 12-15 inches tall.

RHIZO

A major ground cover, ranging in color from burgundy red to a brighter scarlet. Found along riversides and streams, in forest and woodland under heavy shade, and in low-lying, marshy or boggy areas in the north. In most places it has a mossy appearance; in the north coastal area it may send up fine, hairlike processes that resemble fine grass. Forms thick, cushiony mats.

SANTIK

This plant blooms early and continues to bloom throughout the summer. Domesicated plant. Sprawling tangles of purple stems with narrow red-purple leaves. Tiny green flowers are produced at the leaf nodes. When a blossom is touched or visited by a honeyseek, it gives off a strong burst of sweet fragrance. Found bordering fields and gardens. Hedges trimmed to 5-6 feet tall.

SETONY

A common domesticated vegetable, gourd-sized. Knobby, yellow-fleshed tubers produced at the roots of a low bush. Skin is mottled yellow and white when ripe. Texture and protein content similar to potato; smells and tastes a little like pears. Dries well, and is commonly used as a winter vegetable and travel food. Raised in fields and gardens.

SOURSTRAP

A many-branched shrub thickly covered with palm-sized, deeply toothed or serrated orange leaves. Domesticated plant. They are cultivated in most settled areas (they are hardy in the north as well), and a wild type is also relatively common. The leaves are dried to make the tea that is the staple beverage. They contain an alkaloid similar to caffeine and so have a stimulant effect. Grows to about 3 feet.

WINEBERRY

A shrub commonly cultivated for its white berries, produced in the fall, used in making wine. Every farm, estate, and household has its plot of wineberry bushes. In the Oshune area, they are raised on large acreages. The bushes have an attractive, almost globular shape; scarlet flowers are produced in late spring, with the berries forming in mid-summer. Light brown bark, yellow leaves. Grows to about 4 feet.

WIRETHORN

A gray-yellow plant that grows into a twisted mat of stiff, many-jointed stems, with ragged gray-yellow leaves and a mass of sharp spines along every stem and twig. The spines produce a poisonous secretion. A person scratched will not die but suffer a severe skin irritation that can take days, or even weeks, to clear. Found in patches throughout the forests. Also tends to spring up around the stump when a tree is cut down. The bitter smell is a warning to passersby. Can be poisoned with brockney urine.

AUTHOR NOTES

Joan Marie Verba earned a bachelor of physics degree from the University of Minnesota Institute of Technology and attended the graduate school of astronomy at Indiana University, where she was an associate instructor of astronomy for one year. Her first career, as a computer programmer, lasted ten years. After being laid off twice from computer programming jobs, she retrained as an editor and currently works as one. An experienced writer, she is the author of the books *Boldly Writing* (FTL Publications, 1996), and *Voyager: Exploring the Outer Planets* (Lerner Books, 1991), as well as numerous short stories and articles. She is a member of the Science Fiction and Fantasy Writers of America, and the Society of Children's Book Writers and Illustrators.

Tess Meara is a business and technical writer and editor by trade, and freelances widely for electronic and print publications. Tess is a founding member of the National Writers Union Twin Cities Local, and a member of the World Wide Web Artists Consortium, the Society for Technical Communication, and the Horror Writers Association. *Autumn World* is the second genre novel she has published.

Deborah K. Jones is a writer, designer, and fiber artist. Creator of many award-winning costumes, she is a two-time Best in Show winner of the World Science Fiction Convention Masquerade. She has worked as a high school teacher, curriculum researcher, newsletter publisher, database manager, graphic designer, and full-time mother of two. She is married to a professional astronomer and lives in Minnesota. *Autumn World* is her first published work of fiction.

Margaret Howes is a retiree who has become a storyteller in the Society for Creative Anachronism. She has had short stories published in *The Tolkien Scrapbook* and *Sword and Sorceress VIII*, and is the author of the science fiction novel, *The Wrong World* (FTL Publications, 2000). She has drawn maps for the books *Murder at the War* by Mary Monica Pulver, *The Best of Leigh Brackett* (Ballantine/Del Rey, 1977), and the Underwood-Miller edition of *Showboat World* by Jack Vance.

Ruth Berman was conceived in Texas, born in Kentucky, and resident in Minnesota most of the rest of the time. As a middle child in a family that went in for reading aloud, she grew up hearing and speaking a wide variety of books, such as Mother Goose, Shakespeare, Lewis Carroll, L. Frank Baum,

Louisa May Alcott, or Christopher Morley. Her work has appeared in *The Saturday Review, Amazing, Asimov's SF, Weird Tales, The Poet Dreaming in the Artist's House, Burning with a Vision, Aliens and Lovers, The Tolkien Scrapbook, New Worlds, Shadows, Mathenauts, Xanadu,* and many other magazines and anthologies. Her book, *Dear Poppa: The World War II Berman Family Letters* (Minnesota Historical Society Press, 1997), was nominated for a Minnesota Book Award.

All of the above writers are members of the Aaardvark Writing Group, the oldest science fiction writers' workshop in the Twin Cities currently in existence. Founded in 1974 (by Eleanor Arnason and Ruth Berman), it was originally nameless. As other groups became active, a name was needed, and "Aaardvark" (extra "a" intentional) offered alphabetic advantages. The group has seen members through to publication of novels (science fiction, fantasy, mystery), nonfiction books and articles, short stories, and poetry. Several of the Aaardvarks decided to tackle writing a group novel *(Autumn World)* as a project likely to be challenging, instructive, and fun—which it was.